Alice in 9 circles of Wonderhell
catt dahman

Dedication:

To Nic who helped design Alice into a fighting machine
Jeremy, Trevor, Mark, and Stephanie who were always
there.
The S.T.A.L.K.E.R. crew who came up with some crazy
ideas for shops and are super supportive of me.
To Gary Lucas, my editor, for the ideas to go wild with
a story.
To my copy editor who makes my commas behave.

WoNderHeLL

Tammy Dunning

Where am I now? What is this place?
Not knowing how I came to be
in such a scary, evil, tormented space.
What tragedy has befallen me?
The air smells of sulfur. This inferno is hot!
A wicked tea party is taking place on this very spot.
Strange creatures have gathered here,
Demons they must be.
Sitting very nonchalant, sipping on their tea.
A mad man, a rabbit, a cat with a toothy grin,
Red, evil eyes, they turn to me
For in me, they see sin.
The weight of my life is upon me.
Too late to make amends.
Their job is to judge all of those
Whom the devil sends.
I scream, I cry, then turn to run away.
It does no good. I cannot move.
Here is where I'll stay.
"Who are you evil creatures?
What is this ghastly place?
What must I do to be free from you and this horrible
space?"
The mad man answers softly,
His red gaze upon me lies.
His pleasure shines upon his face,
And in it, my own demise.
"We are your jury, child.
And you shall never again be free.
For once you enter through our gates,
Your soul belongs to me.
And as for where we are,
It's really quite easy to tell.
Open your eyes, young Alice. Wake up!
You're in Wonderhell!"

Chapter One: Coral's Diner

My name is Alice, and a few times, people have told me to *go to hell* when they were angry with me. Regrettably, or fortunately, depending on your view, that is more than my destiny: to head down *south;* I have a mission to save the entire world, but I need to begin with the beginning, as acquaintances in Wonderland-hell would say.

When you hear a story and the person telling it begins with, "*It was a normal Saturday night, and I was just a normal person but,*" don't you just want to roll your eyes? Because you know right off the person wasn't that normal if an unbelievable story follows. I felt the same way, so it's okay if you feel that way.

But it was a very normal Saturday night, and I really was a normal girl until the one-eyed, long-fingered, big-eared guy and his friend came into the diner and changed my life.

Like any other Saturday night, tonight we were flooded with hungry people. All day, we had run around the diner, carrying steaming plates of food until we were soaked through with perspiration and needed to cool down and hydrate our bodies.

Now, it was midnight, and I sat in a booth, the same one I sat in every night after the rush was over and the diner was finally closed. Four others sat with me while we drank sodas and ice water and let the smoke from our cigarettes drift upwards to the ceiling where the residue collected with oils and smoke from the food we had served. My feet ached, so I wriggled my toes to get the feeling back into them.

"Go smoke outside," Coral yelled, just as he did every night, telling us that we needed to go outside for our bad habits, but he wasn't a ball-breaker kind of boss. He knew we would stay seated at the booth while we smoked and rested before trudging off to our homes.

Then, he finished up in the kitchen, maybe getting his first chance to have a bite of food.

He banged pot and pans around, as he made sure his kitchen was pristine for the next day.

"Okay," I yelled back, but we didn't get up and go outside. It was too warm and muggy, and the air conditioning inside felt good as it dried our sweat with its chill.

"Coral said to go outside," Cory said lazily.

"Yep, he did," I said.

Coral was a fair boss, as well as being calm and friendly to us. He expected good service, honesty, dependability, and hard work from those of us he employed, and in return, he paid very good wages, showed us full respect, and genuinely cared about our families and about us. We could go to him like a dad with any qualms or problems we had.

He actually paid the best of anyone in town, but he was very choosey about whom he hired.

Coral was one guy in town whom everyone liked a lot. He was a go-to-guy, and when he expressed an opinion, people listened and cared.

He was a huge-built African American man with a booming voice. He used to be some big time football star but ruined his knees and came back to his small town birthplace and opened his diner: *Coral's Diner*. Original, huh?

There weren't many places to eat in town, but his food was really good, there was a lot of the food, and it was priced well.

The place was always full, and he did a steady business. He served home cooked meals such as meatloaf, enchiladas, or ham steak and served with good vegetables such as mashed potatoes, fresh green beans, fried okra, and seasoned cabbage. Fruit from the farmer's market across the street went into his cobblers: peach, apple, and blackberry.

He had learned excellent recipes from his mother and grandmother, and no one got preservatives and junk in his food.

From 4:30 pm-senior-citizen specials until 10:30 pm-the-late-night crowd, the diner was steadily swamped by people coming in to eat. They all wanted burgers: double beef, bacon and cheese, mushroom and onion, avocado and salsa with jalapeños, and every other combination imaginable.

Luckily, we never got tired of the scents of those burgers, as they always smelled mouth-watering; unfortunately, in the rush, we never had time to eat them.

The bad part was we were tired; the good part was time had flown by, and we got bonuses for waiting over-flow; Coral was fair that way.

"I'm tired. Why did the school band all want extra fries tonight?" Dana grumbled. She was the lead waitress and my best friend, "People at every table ordered extra fries after they got their meals, so I had to run for more fries and refigure the bills."

After a marathon band practice at the high school, the entire group, thirty in all with ferocious appetites for burgers, double fries, milkshakes, and brownies with ice cream, milkshakes, and brownies with ice cream stormed in the diner.

"Because Coral added the damned sweet potato fries to the menu and they love those," Pax said, laughing, "They are fantastic, by the way, in case you were too busy to eat one."

He was the new cook who worked alongside of Coral, easy going and dependable, and he and Coral had spent hours coming up with the special recipe for the new fries. They had just been added to the menu: were cut from sweet potatoes, soaked in milk and spices, battered thickly with a mixture of flour and more spices, then fried crisp, and finally drained so they weren't greasy. They were a little sweet, a lot hot and spicy, and as popular as his home made spicy, garlic-dill pickles, which also vanished. During that night alone, we sold an additional ten jars of the special pickles at fifteen dollars a jar!

I didn't bother to tell Pax that Annie, Dana, and I had dinner on the run while we worked: pickles, sweet potato fries, and jalapeño poppers. If we told him we had eaten his special fries and loved them, he would question us forever to make sure they were prefect. I hid a smile.

Later, when Pax was gone, I would feel a twinge of sadness that I never bragged on his fries, but right then, I could not have dreamed where my destiny would lead me.

In Coral's diner, there was no drama: no whining or shirking of duties, no taking advantage of others, and no complaining about problems; if you didn't follow those rules, you wouldn't last long. You got what you put into your work.

That's why we were there. It was enough to have all that drama and back stabbing in our personal lives; we didn't want it at our jobs, too. We got along fantastically.

"The band uniforms this year look stupid," Dana said.

"They do every year," I added. I would make fun of their uniforms but had a healthy respect for their hard work and the band director's leadership since they played strong, recognizable tunes with few participants.

"You're jealous 'cause you can't wear one instead of your diner uniform," Pax laughed at Dana, teasing her.

"Whatever," she said, rolling her eyes. Her *uniform* was her work shirt, light blue, and embroidered with her name and worn with a tight, short denim skirt and high-topped sneakers.

She got better tips than me because she wore her shirt tighter and unbuttoned two buttons down. As long as we wore our work shirts, Coral didn't care what we paired it with as long as it was clean and neatly pressed every day.

"My feet hurt," I said. I leaned back against the wall, sitting in the booth sideways, with my feet propped up on Cory's lap. He shrugged, letting my sneakers bang down onto the seat as he got up to get a refill, "Ouch," I snarled.

Annie giggled at us. Annie was a great person, humble and sweet, hardworking, and a good friend. She was a far better person than the rest of us, with dreams in her eyes, and she did weekly good deeds.

She drove me crazy sometimes because she was such a good person and made such an effort to be one; she went out of her way just to find ways to be nice. She might stop at a house and help the owner weed a garden, take soup to someone ill, or take empty toilet paper rolls to the school's art teacher, simply to make someone smile.

I admired that and was frightened by such effort.

Like most of the rest, I worked double shifts for the money and because that's just who I am: Coral could always depend on me. That was my good deed.

I worked double shifts seven days a week when Dana was away, and I would take a bullet before letting Coral down. It was better to know I was there and handling the business professionally and honestly than to worry that anyone else might let him down the tiniest bit.

One frown and I would move the earth to fix things for my boss.

"We're closed," Cory said loudly.

Cory was one I often wanted to slap but never had good cause or the energy. He was a pain in the ass with smart remarks but always dependable and often even nice. That his smart-assed remarks were usually warranted drove me nuts but in a good way, as if he were an irritating brother.

"No kidding?" I asked.

He pointed to the door as he filled his glass with ice, "I'm telling those guys."

We looked around. See? He had irritated me and again; he was right. I couldn't win.

At the glass door stood a fellow who was wearing black clothing and had an eye patch over his right eye like a goofy pirate. He ignored Cory and waved at us, motioning to the lock on the door. He was tall, over six feet and with an average build. He wore too-tight, skinny-legged jeans and a tight tee shirt. He had long, dark hair and reminded me of a rock and roll singer, maybe one of those death metal guys that never got past the 1980s.

"Let them in," Coral yelled from the kitchen. Sometimes, it was if the man had x-ray vision and knew what was going on even when he couldn't see the front.

Once, he said we needed to fill all the ketchup bottles during a really fast- paced, huge rush, and we started to argue that we didn't have time and that the bottles were fine, but sure enough, they were all low.

He didn't look out front, but Coral knew. He said it was because he knew how many burgers he had cooked that night and because people insisted on ruining them with ketchup. He could hear a crash and know which one of us had dropped dishes, too. He said Dana dropped them the hardest, which was funny.

We wouldn't have let them in if Coral hadn't directed us to.

Anyway, Cory frowned and walked over to let the pirate/death metal man and his friend inside, unlocking and relocking the door with no obvious interest in the guys.

I will say this for Cory, if they had been dangerous, Cory would have sensed it, would have them disarmed, and would have them on the floor at once. Cory was protective of us, and he could sense trouble, maybe even smell it on a person.

Cory came back, lifted my feet, and settled back into the booth with my feet again hanging across his lap because he wanted to sit in my space.

Cory was telling us, before he got up for his refill, about a car he was restoring and jumped right back into the boring details as soon as he sat down and lit another cigarette. We didn't care about his car and the engine he was putting it in; his voice was a drone of monotony, hence why I wanted to slap him at times.

"That's the last thing you need," the newcomer wearing the eye patch said, looking right at me and wrinkling his nose as he saw my hand flick an ash into the ashtray on the table.

He waved at the smoke dramatically. Maybe the man was an old rock-and-roller and had played at halftime when Coral was playing a football bowl game; I could imagine the man in black, hopping about with a guitar.

The other man wasn't dressed like the first; he wore jeans, flat roper boots, a tee shirt, and a cowboy hat. He looked slightly annoyed with his companion and shyly smiled. He was plain until then, but the smile lit his face and made his eyes twinkle, but he didn't seem the type to smile a lot. Just a feeling I had.

A cat was with them, and he looked as if he were grinning some of the time; he was a cocky little cat, grey and white and very fluffy.

"Coral, you gotta a couple of visitors," I yelled. What I didn't need after a long, hard shift waiting tables and getting band kids extra fries was some weird looking man, expounding on my tobacco habit, especially in front of everyone else.

Anyone's calling attention to me was one of my worst fears.

"Alice, Coral knows we're here. But we really came to see you."

I felt a huge, heavy lump in my stomach.

Now, imagine you are already tired and cranky, it's after work, and a man comes in, makes a negative statement about your habits, and then says he's there to see you. Can you see my issue?

Why would he be there to see me since we obviously have nothing in common and don't know one another? If he wanted a date, he was out of luck. *Please don't let him ask* me out, I prayed.

I didn't date because no one really interested me.Dana said it was because I didn't take to small town boys I had grown up with and that I should meet a man from outside town. They seemed as single-minded and boring as the boys I already knew, so what was the point?

This guy certainly didn't interest me. He was abnormal but not plain, dressed funny, and was cryptic, so he was easy to strike through as a possibility. I didn't give people chances. If you never depend on anyone and never give him a chance, you will never be let down.

Dana said that was antisocial.

I just didn't like anything that might be a change or effort.I was boring, plain, and normal as could be. I took classes for college online, worked in a diner, lived at home with my parents, and lived in that small town where nothing out of the ordinary ever happened.

And I liked it that way.

Adding sweet potato fries to the menu was almost more than I could take, and Coral had to tell me calmly and allow me to get used to the idea before I could handle that change.

I mean I had to say, "Regular or sweet potato fries, batter with spices and fried golden?" Then, people might ask questions, think about it, or ask my opinion. It was too much responsibility.

After I finished some online work, I was going to commute to college, (and not go to college parties, join a stupid sorority, go to silly sports events, or anything of the sort), get my college degree, come back, and teach at the school I had attended.

Teaching seemed the least exciting, least adventurous route I could pick, and that was my choice. I didn't intend to date, get married, or have children.

Do you see how uninspired I was? Good. I want to make it very clear that I was very average in looks, personality, and aspirations. Below average in some of those, in fact. I enjoyed solitude and the quiet side of life. I brushed my dark hair into the same ponytail every day after using the same shampoo and never had to wonder if my hair looked different, good, or bad. I was the same each and every day.

If one actually did anything, especially anything differently, there was room for disappointment or harm.

"Why?" I asked the man with the eye patch. Asking him that question was a big deal for me; I hadn't shown that much enthusiasm and interest in ages. I only asked, really, so I could hear his reason and then tell him to move on that I wasn't interested.

"We'll wait on Coral," the man said. That drove me almost insane. We had to wait. See? If you ask a question or show interest, you'll get burned every time. There's no winning.

Then he told us his name was Danny as he pulled a chair from under a table, flipped it around, and sat on it backwards so his chin rested on the high metal bar that was the back of the chair.

I was quite sure his tight pants would burst a seam, but he didn't indicate it had happened. The other man sat down next to him; his name was Virgil, which was a fitting name for a cowboy. They said the cat was Limmerfer, an odd name.

"Well, have yourself a seat," Pax said as he locked eyes with me.

I shrugged. I didn't ask the men to sit with us.

Danny picked up the paper covering from one of our straws and began meticulously folding it like an accordion, and that's when we noticed his fingers were very long, too long.

I blinked my eyes and looked again to be sure, but yes, each finger had an extra joint. Imagine a normal hand, or look at your own. Now, imagine that between your first and second joints is another finger bone and joint, about half as long as the second one.

I'll wait until you do that.

Right. So it looked kind of strange but also cool in a way. He caught us looking at his long fingers and grinned, "I know. It's pretty awesome, isn't it?"

"Awesomesauce," Dana said, kind of rudely. She was making fun of his way of speaking. She had gone off to college for a few years and then returned, claiming she hated the whole ordeal.

She claimed she would rather wait tables the rest of her life than go to another party or sit in a class of a hundred students, listening to a dull lecture.

I had missed her when she was away, but she hadn't called or even kept in touch as she had promised when she was gone.

Once back, she didn't talk much about what all she had done while she was away but just said she hated it. But since she had left the town and lived in another place, she was as close to a worldly friend as we had. If she thought his terminology was uncool, then it probably was.

Dana deliberately blew smoke close to Danny and flicked her ashes so she missed the ashtray, but the man never said a word to her. He watched me light up and made me feel creepy-crawly. We didn't know what to talk about now that two strange men and a cat had joined us at our table.

CHApter 2:ErraNd: to HeLL aNd BaCK

Coral came from the kitchen, wiping his hands on a towel and grinning until he saw Danny. The grin kind of rolled off his face, and he looked more resigned than glad to see the man. With a sigh, Coral sat in the booth beside us and peered over the back. He pushed the table to the other side so he could fit his still-massive frame comfortably in the space.

"Hi ya, Danny," Coral said.

Danny grinned, "Why, hello, Coral. You knew I'd be here. Be happy."

That kind of worried me. It was something eerie like a mob member might say. Was Danny in the mafia? Nah, not dressed that way, he couldn't be. "Danny said he came to see me," I told Coral.

"Yep, I was expecting him and Virgil. Kind of was hoping he might forget to show up or change his mind," Coral said, as if Danny couldn't hear us.

We glanced at Danny to see how he took that comment, but he didn't seem to care. He kept folding his little paper and testing it. Virgil looked more interested, considering every word, and he watched me a lot, pretending not to.

"Well, tell me why you're here, Danny. I wanna head on home and get some sleep," I said, "I don't like surprises."

Danny dropped the paper and tilted his head, "Now that we're all here, I can tell you that I came to get you so you can run a most important errand."

Cory and Pax almost fell over laughing, and Annie giggled again. Dana and I looked at one another until I began laughing, too,

"Oh really? Well, I'm not energetic enough to run an errand for you, so you better ask someone else, Danny. Sorry."All this drama about some errand? How silly. And you'd think maybe it was some big secretive errand such as running drugs or moonshine for all the drama, but then I knew Coral wouldn't be a part of that.

I did manage to catch Coral's eyes, wondering what part he played in all this. I wasn't bothered by the fact that we had all laughed in Danny's face but did wonder why Coral was part of this. Had it all ended there and had I never been given an explanation, I would have been fine. See? Totally uninterested about life.

Coral nodded, "I guess there's no easy way for Danny to ask you, but he's trying, Alice. Hear him out anyway, okay? Let him tell you about this errand because it really is critical."

Danny leaned forward as if he had a great secret to share, "Alice, we need you to run a very important errand to hell and back."

I made a little noise. Well, that was strange thing to say to me. I almost laughed. How dramatic. *To hell and back.* "Well, I see. So, really…what errand and where?"

Danny cocked his head to one side, "As I said. It's to *hell* and back. Quite literally, we need you to enter hell, deliver something to someone, and then, well, hopefully if everything goes right, to come back; then, you can go on just as you are."

"I dunno. Hell, huh?" I laughed. "That's a long way, I bet."

"I know a shortcut," said Danny and winked.

"Coral, come on. This isn't like you to joke around," I berated my boss. He was a nice man, sometimes kind of funny for an old guy (he was fortyish which to me was ancient) and always laughed, but he wasn't a practical joker, so this was out of character. Why were they pulling a prank on me of all people? It wasn't as if I were the sort to appreciate it. *What was going on?*

Coral studied his fingernails, "It's not a joke. Danny thinks I can get you prepared physically to run the errand. I remember how to work out."

"To run an errand to hell? Work out? As in weights and running? No way. It's me you are talking to." I finished his sentence, yawning.

As you have no doubt realized, I was happily bored, still, and simply not interested in this discussion; I wanted it to be over so I could get some sleep. This was a waste of time.

11

"Exactly," said Danny.

"Does anyone else feel like this conversation is a little weird? I mean, if I were stoned or drunk…maybe…." Cory said.

"I know it's strange, and, of course, you don't believe this is true, but Danny and Virgil really are here to ask for the help. Alice, you don't have to do it. It's totally up to you, but if you decide to do it, I could help you train for it," Coral told me.

I looked at Virgil. He didn't say anything about all this, but he listened and nodded sometimes; he watched me carefully. It made me feel weird to have him *appraising* me.

"Slow down. Why ask Alice? And why would she have to train? What kind of errand? And why does it have to be run? You can't just ask without giving us some details," Dana said, practical as always. I could see that, unfortunately, she was interested in hearing this out.

"Ah, yes, details," Danny said.

I swear I thought I saw his right ear twitch. Virgil saw it twitch too because he was looking at his buddy when it happened. When he glanced at me, he knew I had seen, too, and as we met eyes, we both suppressed laughs.

"There was a slight mistake made. It really never happens, but this time…it did," Danny told us.

Coral nodded.

"Many of those who go to hell are quite deserving of the punishment and are very evil people whom you know as mass murderers, serial killers, child molesters, and rapists. Then, you get the little people who are kind of bad like politicians, suicides without cause, dinosaurs, thieves, hookers, drug users, long-tongued liars, and false prophets. Next, you have those who serve tea improperly, adulterers, ramblers and gamblers, and wife beaters."

"Dinosaurs?" Pax burst out.

"Tea?" Annie asked

Danny nodded solemnly, "The stubby armed ones are particularly evil. Dinos, I mean. The tea thing would take hours to explain, and hot tea and cups and…well…it has to do with a lot of other issues. Spiders and scorpions, snakes, and other beasties are there, too."

We looked at one another in surprise.

"All of that…well, there have been a lot of people over the years, so hell is very full. Too full, in fact."

"Hell can get too full?" Pax asked Danny.

"Certainly. The last few years have been busy with intakes, but you know the saying '*when there is no more room in hell, the dead shall walk the earth*'? It's like that.

CHapter 3: TecHNicaLLy, HeLL IS FuLL: ONe Too MaNy

Hell is full, and some are worried that the dead will have to walk the earth; this could get complicated and messy." Danny waved his hands as if that explained everything to us.

"Oh, like zombies?" My head buzzed with all that he had said. I was really still back on dinosaurs and tea, but the dead walking around jumped ahead in my mind.

"Sort of," Virgil told Cory. He hadn't said much, but he had a very nice voice, such as the kind that you would want to read a bedtime story to you.

Danny continued. He said the *Big Boss Down Under(*which was how he called Satan so as not to call his name aloud) was working on an expansion, and it would hold a few million more souls, but for now, everything was on hold because technically, hell was full. The *waiting room* was really getting stuffy.

A big debate was going on about whether the dead could walk the earth yet. Both sides were waiting for there to be a decision made.

"Can't…you know…?" Cory pointed upwards. "Decide it?"

"You'd think there would be rules set for everyone to follow, even the angels, because after all, if He didn't make rules and then follow them, then we'd have general chaos. Even the *Big Boss Down Under, BBDU,* appreciates that part."

Danny explained more,"A girl was deposited in hell, and she was the final soul or the soul that *broke the camel's back*, so to speak. She was the one who caused hell to technically be full."

"He said it wasn't literally full as in wall-to-wall stuffed, but full as in some mathematical equation that was complicated; he pointed out that math was hell, and we nodded in agreement on that part."

" Because of the circumstances," he said, "there was some question as to whether she, the final girl, should have gone to hell or been forgiven after doing some time in purgatory, or at least that's what the Holy Attorneys claimed."

"Heaven has attorneys?" Cory asked.

"Sure. But few actually. Hell gets almost all of them," Danny said.

To make it all simpler, the *Holy Attorneys* decided that they would get the girl out, and then there would be one space open, renovations could take place, and the dead would stay down below. That would easily solve all the issues. However, there were some more rules that interfered with that.

"More rules," Dana rolled her eyes.

"Souls can't just pop in and out of hell like that. People can't be allowed to just...*leave*. Think of the mess that would cause if a soul could walk out at any time, even with permission. Utter massive chaos, I tell you. We'd have a real mess. Even *BBDU* doesn't like that idea."

"Makes sense," I said. I guessed that even in hell, there had to be rules and organization.

Danny nodded, "So a certain key is required for her to leave. Therein lies the problem, see? Someone has to go down there and give it to her so she can use it.As you know, *BBDU* and his demons are very powerful, and so are the souls down there. It wouldn't be safe for one of the Holy Ones to run around in hell because they would be targets, and there is no way we could cover up their auras."

"Auras?" Annie asked.

"Yes. We all have them. Remember haloes: the light around people's heads? That is really an exaggeration, but auras are haloes."

"You have one; everyone has one when he is alive or holy. Some are golden or white, and some are colored if the person has a special gift. It's an electrometric field; that is all."

"Really? We have them?" I spun to stare hard at Dana, and then Coral; I saw nothing. The others didn't have anything around their heads either. Stupid man probably was just saying it to confuse me."

" Alice, yours is very bright white. It's the brightest, biggest electromagnetic field, or aura, we have seen. It means you have a very powerful spirit, but it also means that physically, you are lacking."

"Well, thanks so much," I sneered at Virgil. *What an asshole.* Like he had to tell me that in front of everyone?

"They aren't protected? The Angels?" Dana asked, changing the subject.

"Of course, they are, but not there they aren't.

When the *Big Boss* threw *BBDU* out, well, He gave the guy dominion, see? Rules.

If the top guys appeared in hell to get the girl out, they'd be seen by millions of demons and attacked. Way too risky. I mean Michael could lead them, and they would win, but it would be a big battle, and everything would be a mess for a long time.

Right now, only a few of us know who she is. If *BBDU* found out, or when he finds out, he'll send his minions to tempt her, and we won't be able to get her back then and well...."

"The dead will inherit the earth," Cory said, "I get it. Zombies. That's really wacked. If the chick stays in hell, we get a zombie apocalypse."

Danny reminded us that action would be unpleasant for everyone, but Cory loved zombie books and movies and was really into role-playing games on the computer that killed zombies.

Danny quoted from a series called *Z is for Zombie* all the time, he claimed that was the end-all about zombie invasions, and he used it to prepare. Cory was kind of excited about a fight with Zs.

"This isn't like books and movies. They stink, Cory. Yuk. And we'd all have to fight instead of working here and eating sweet potato fries," Annie said.

Cory looked askance, "That would suck."

Pax broke in, "And you came to ask Alice to take the key to the girl so she can get out. If she does, then hell expands, and we are zombie free."

"That's pretty much how it is," Virgil said.

Dana shook her head, "Again, why Alice? And that sounds dangerous to me."

Well, it did to me as well. Movies showed hell as a burning place full of terrible monsters. I told Danny how I felt.

Danny shrugged, "Fire is fairly limited to the Eternal Pit of Fire, as opposed to the Eternal Pit of Shit or the Eternal Pit of Puke. Those who are tossed in those places are in a world of sh... well, you get what I mean."

"It's terribly dangerous," Coral said, "and I did say to you Alice surely doesn't *have* to do this mission. In fact, I would say to tell Danny no, but Alice has to hear the facts and decide for herself."

"Free will," Annie added.

Danny used his hand as a pistol and pointed at her as if he were thumbing the hammer back. He made a clucking noise, "You are sharp, Annie."

I didn't believe this, but then I wasn't really into all the reasons why I didn't believe it.

The first thought in my head was that if it were true, I was about the most unlikely person on earth to ask to do such a thing.

Some might be curious, but I wasn't in the least. I told Danny, "I'm not a likely candidate, am I? Seriously. If you knew me...."

"We do know you, Alice. We have researched you, looked at pictures, and read about you. We know you better than you know yourself in some ways," Virgil told us.

"Creepy," I said.

Chapter 4: Alice's Story

I kicked off my sneakers and waved my white socks at Cory, begging him to rub my feet since I was sitting here listening to this, entertaining him. I texted home to say I was working late so Dad would go on to bed.

While I did that, Coral got Danny some vegetable juice and refilled our glasses. He handed Limmerfer a little bowl of milk.

After my shifts on Friday and Saturday nights, my dad always stayed up late to rub my feet.I would sit at one end of the sofa munching popcorn or nachos and sipping cola while he rubbed my feet, alternating stories he told me.

For a while, night after night, he cautioned about my not caring for my feet properly as only a podiatrist can while listing every bone in my foot and toes.

Then, he would tell me funny stories about when I was a baby and then back to cautionary tales based on foot problems he saw every day in the city.

Dad could list every popular style shoe and tell me exactly how each deformed women's feet. He could figure out the pounds of pressure on a foot by looking at the shoe, guessing at the woman's weight, and doing the math. Mom and I wore Birkenstocks or sneakers so he didn't fuss at us.

I always went to bed relaxed with less-sore feet than before he worked on them. Good thing I wasn't ticklish. Mom always flitted in and out of the den, asking questions about who had eaten what that night and laughing at me when I yelped as Dad hit a particularly tender spot.

My parents are the best.

Cory gave up complaining and rubbed my feet. He wasn't an expert, and it wasn't nearly soothing enough, but it was better than aching.

To retaliate a little, he asked, "Yeah, why Alice? She's clumsy and out of shape. Especially her feet."

I dug a heel into his crotch, making him wince.

Danny put took a long drink of his juice, smacked his lips, and kind of wiggled his nose, "Many reasons. For one, I already have said Alice has an aura like no other. I don't have anything to do with that but only can say hers is strong and bright."

"Yay me," I sulked.

"Another reason is Dana. If you recall, a little over a year ago, she was in the hospital."

Dana shifted uncomfortably, "Let's not go into that. It was a bad time for me, and I...."

No doubt she was remembering the pain she had been through. After returning from college, she suffered a massive pelvic infection and hemorrhaging that had almost taken her life.

I drove to the city every other day to see her, sitting by her bed, hoping and praying she would survive. It was a close call before the antibiotics took effect and two weeks passed before she was released to come home.

"As you recall, you asked for a few favors," Virgil told me.

"What? You mean you want me to repay for *Dana*? I don't think it works that way."

Keep in mind, I didn't believe him but was arguing the one point I could, "I mean, yes, I asked a favor, and I will repay but *come on....*"

"And Dana should pay, not Alice, I mean if this were real, she should," Cory said, "no offense, Dana."

"I vote Dana does it, too," Pax said.

"Thanks a lot. But he said Alice, not me," Dana said.

"You don't get to vote," Coral told us, "and Danny, that isn't fair. You aren't supposed to add that in."

Danny shrugged, "Sorry. She asked why...."

Coral nodded, "And the answer is because you are dependable, honest, and loyal, and once you set your mind to something, you do it, Alice. I think underneath your ineptitude and apathy, you have the makings of a fine warrior. You've just never had a goal."

A warrior? That was funny. And by the way, I didn't give a flying rat's ass about goals. Seriously. I didn't know if that were a compliment or not, what Coral said. I doubted it was.

Cory laughed at me, "Warrior. Rip and tear, Alice…."

Cory asked what reward I got if I did it. He was always about the rewards.

Danny blinked, "Well, I could maybe get you a small reward, Alice, if you insisted on one," he said it as if I had asked, which I hadn't. I kicked Cory.

I told Danny that I couldn't neglect work to traipse through hell, and in actuality I wasn't interested in the adventure, but Coral considerately said I could take time off.

I said I wasn't in shape; Coral said he could get me ready in four weeks, in plenty of time for a trip *south*. I said I was terrible with directions and would get lost in hell, and Coral offered to accompany me on my excursion.

I couldn't catch a break.

I said I didn't want to go. There. That was the nut of the matter.

Danny nodded and stood, "Then, my work here is finished. Thank you for hearing us out anyway, Alice."

"That's all? You'll find someone else?" I asked. That was easy. If this were real, which it was not, they could find someone else and save the world, and my life could go on as plainly as before they showed up. Fantastic.

"Oh, no, there *is* no one else. You were actually our second choice since the first choice got into some trouble and doesn't have a clean enough slate to possibly go and make it back out."

Second choice? Well.

" Alice, your apathy and lack of adventure has reserved you from getting into the majority of trouble that teens and young adults get into; you are nearly faultless as far as having no bad tick marks on your tally sheet."

"Then, you missed when I cheated on a math quiz in tenth grade, shoplifted a candy bar, but returned it the next day…oh, and I lied to Ronnie, the police officer about my blinkers once," I confessed.

"I'll go," Cory said.

"Thank you, Cory. That's kind of you to offer, but you have quite a few black marks against you, and I don't think you could do this alone. Had Alice taken the quest and you had gone along, I could have gotten you a fresh slate, but she has said, 'No.' "

"Thanks a lot, Alice." Cory pushed my feet away. "Now, I am stuck with black marks I can't get rid of. Are they serious?"

"Ummm. I'm not supposed to say, but you are at the edge. If I could gamble and not get a tick mark for it, I would bet that you, Cory, will end up...ummm, down south."

"Great, I'm going to hell, Alice."

I clenched my jaw. This was the most insane conversation I had ever been a part of, and Cory 's going along with it made me almost bothered.

Why was it my fault he was going to hell?

"Could I get my marks wiped away?" Dana asked, "I'll go if you want."

I saw her bottom lip was actually quivering. What the hell? Pardon the pun. Dana never got upset, but she looked flustered by this. Scared.

"Sorry. Again, only if you went along with Alice." Danny gave Coral a sad look. "Sorry, Coral. Maybe you'll find another way to get *your* records expunged."

"This isn't fair to try to guilt me into it with my friends," I argued. I looked at Cory and amended my statement, "Well, with some of my friends and some just people I work with." Dana's frightened look worried me. Danny said Coral had black marks as well? *For what?*

I saw something that caught my attention and motioned Danny to lean closer to me and show me his hand. If he had refused, I was just concerned enough now that I would have jumped up and grabbed his hand.

Remember I mentioned his fingers had extra joints? What I saw was this: his hands also were smooth on the palms except for a few round callused areas, like the pad of a dog's foot. Or like a cat's foot. Or like a rabbit's foot.As I traced the odd hands with my fingertips, curious for the first time in my life, Danny pulled out an old-fashioned pocket watch that he looked at before shoving it back into the pocket of his pants.

"Oh, dear, oh dear, *I shall be too late*," he said, and this time, I was sure his right ear wiggled a little.

Virgil nodded sagely.

The pocket watch, an antique, I thought, was so out of place and stranger than the multi-jointed fingers, twitching ear, and Danny's eye patch.

Chapter 5: Let's Get the Girl and Save the World

I sat back all at once, my jaw hanging open. I am sure I had never expressed that amount of shock. All at once, I *knew* this was not a joke or a figment of someone's imagination. It hit me full force that everything was absolutely true.

Now that, as you can bet, put a little different spin on everything I had heard. "Wait, Danny, when the dead walk the earth, what will they do?"

"Ummm. They will eat the living. Didn't you see George Romero's film about that? Quite well done and frightening."

"It was just a movie about zombies."

Limmerfer chuffed; it was as if he were laughing.

"Oh, it was supposed to show a warning; no wonder people didn't take it to heart if you thought it was just a movie. It makes me wonder why the Holy Movie Makers worked so hard on that if no one believed."

"*Holy Movie Makers*? They exist?"

"A few. The other side gets them a lot of the time, too," Danny muttered. "And to answer your question, they'll attack people, bite them, and feast on their guts, and they'll spread the rot until everyone is consumed or is walking around in a zombie daze. That was just like the movie showed."

"So if I don't go, then I'll wind up battling zombies? Here? That sucks, Danny. Some of these rules aren't fair. I'm tempted to go with you, find *BBDU*, and stake him through the gut."

"Is that *interest* from our Alice?" Cory laughed.

Danny and Virgil looked questioningly at me. On the other side, Coral sat up again, hope filling his face.

"My mom and dad could never handle zombies. They would really lose it," I said, "and I have the greatest parents on earth."

"Yes, you do. They have no tick marks against them," Virgil said, nodding.

"Well?" Coral asked.

I smiled a little, "Well, count me in. Let's get the girl out and save the world."

To my surprise, Cory, Annie, Dana, and Coral cheered.

Danny grinned wider, and I noticed how long his front teeth were. Really, he was an odd looking fellow. Danny and Coral put their heads together, planning something about my training that I chose to ignore because it sounded a lot like work to me.

Annie and Pax asked if they could go, and I said sure, the more the merrier, I thought.

Annie whispered to me that she had a little problem sometimes with taking things, things that weren't hers, and she might want to wipe off a few black marks on her own record.

It sounded as if no one were going actually to help me and protect me; they all wanted to clear their own records and go for themselves. That was all right because other than my parents, no one particularly did anything to help me, so it wasn't anything I expected. *But still.*

"I like that pocket watch," I said softly.

Annie whispered a giggle back to me, "Me, too."

If it went missing, I knew where to look. My adventure was about to begin.

Chapter 6: Training

I've never been the athletic type. Frankly, I prefer to watch other people sweat. That's why I have ten, okay, I won't lie, twenty pounds to work off in the next four weeks, which is a lot of weight. I wasn't chunky, but I was soft if you get my meaning. I had pudge around my middle.

Coral began by making us run.

"Run? No. I can't." I had driven over to the park and scuffed the ground with my sneakers, making circles in the dirt. Coral motioned me to join him, and for a little while, we walked. Then, we jogged, and I groaned and complained. Jogging bounced my head around.

Coral stopped and had me stretch for a while. I raised my arms and pushed them back and forwards like he showed me. I kicked my legs out to the side and to the back with Coral steadying me like a ballet dancer. I rotated my body. Ouch. Everything pulled.

We ran a little ways. We stretched again. I was young and had few bad habits, and my body remembered it was young, basically well fed with good food, and had stamina from long hours on my feet.

The next day, we ran more and lifted weights even though I was sore. Do you think Coral cared or accepted my excuses? Nope.

I hated every second. Coral called it endurance, and I called it torture because half the time, I puked.

He said it was hard on him as well since he hadn't trained in a long time. Ha ha. He deserved the pain.

Sometimes Pax ran with me, and sometimes one of the others had to do it. Luckily, the more I ran, the better I was, and after two weeks, I didn't throw up all the time but still huffed and puffed.

I wore leg weights strapped to my ankles almost always, so when I removed them to run, I felt lighter on my feet. I was running faster and longer. Sometimes the cat, Limmerfer, ran with me, which was very queer, but then he wasn't like any cat I had ever met.

Oh, I gave up smoking, too.

Coral put me on strict diet, but I loved it. I could have all the raw vegetables I wanted, so I gorged on tomatoes and cucumbers. I became a gazpacho addict. I learned to eat carrots dipped in Coral's famous salsa; *Danny was big-time into carrots*. I ate Coral's garlic dill pickles, black beans, and lean proteins. I had no sugar and almost no carbs on my new diet.

Coral managed my physical abilities, teaching me how to kick and fight, which I have to admit, was fun.

Danny said I would have some challenges, and I learned all kinds of fancy moves to kick ass. I learned a great tuck and roll that I enjoyed doing all over the place. My dad could only wonder when I did my rolls across the front lawn.

Danny told me from minute one that he had some magic tricks up his sleeve, but I didn't believe him, as you know I didn't. I figured it was pretend.

Danny fed me special vitamins that increased my energy level, and he had me lie on the grass or floor or wherever was handy, and he massaged my temples and softly talked really low. Now, I know you're thinking about those weird fingers rubbing on my temples and shivering because yes, I got the heebie jeebies when he first did it.

Dana and the rest were around, so I gave it a try even if it were eerie.

I had to lie on my back in a dimly lit room while he rubbed my head. I got sleepy and drifted half-asleep. I guess it was hypnosis, but it was relaxing.

I always felt refreshed afterwards, and Danny told me…get this…that he was implanting memories of fighting and beating up demons and bad guys. Crazy, huh?

But each time I practiced with Coral, I was better and better at blocking punches and could finally take him down within seconds. Danny said my head and body remembered (falsely in my opinion) that I was a warrior.

Me? A warrior? Too funny.

Danny turned out to be like a fussy aunt, and he measured me a lot and complained about my hair and said I was two inches too short.

I am only five feet five. My hair is dull black, but Danny sat and brushed it when he was preparing me for my trip, and somehow my hair began to fall glossy and rich on my shoulders. That made me happy because I knew that it looked wonderful.

He promised me a great surprise on the day I was to go to hell.

Virgil spent a lot of time giving me pep talks and holding my hair back for me when I puked from working out. He was the one I confided my fears too because he didn't try to change my mind but agreed it was a daunting, dangerous task before me.I had to be at the top of my game or I would fail, not only for my friends and me but also for the world.

Gee, no pressure.

Chapter 7: My Team: Ready For Hell

I liked Danny. He was funny and interesting. He was an enigma. I liked my team. Virgil, though, he was one I didn't know how to assign an emotion to. I was frightened because I felt, in many ways, I needed him as a friend; he was filling a void in my life that I had not known was there.

One afternoon, we took off and went to a movie, just us. We needed the break. I pretended it was a date and laughed and had fun, and you know what? It *was* fun. He knew me well. I felt comfortable. It was just nice to pretend everything was normal but better than just normal and I was out with a handsome man who liked me in that way.

Maybe that is silly, but it was *my* silly.

I was prepared as possible.

We met in the park where I often trained. Annie, Pax, Coral, Dana, and Cory were there, ready to go. I admired their outfits, even if I weren't into fashion. They had on leather pants or shorts, jackets and boots, except for Danny who wore a longer jacket and a very British-looking, grey plaid vest and a top hat. It was better than the tight pants and rocker tee shirt.

His right ear waggled.

Virgil looked like a western gunfighter, only hotter with his leather, boots, and hat. But I tried not to notice that part.

Limmerfer had been brushed until he was glossy; his white patches almost glowed. Across his upper back, around his chest, and under his front legs, he wore a cute tiny vest with tiny pockets, and he didn't mind it at all.

They looked like fighters.

Danny handed me a big, heavy box, and despite myself, I felt a thrill of excitement. Inside, neatly folded was the outfit I would wear. "Let's get you changed and then into this box," he said as he motioned to another box, "we'll get you set with weapons."

I was excited. Danny motioned me into a small blue tent.

I hope you can see why I had changed my views. I was interested, and I worked hard to train. Why? Because I had to. If not me, there was no one else who could take my place. Always, I had to do things *because there was no one else.*

Dana had to help me get into the corset. It was well made and fit me like a glove, white with black trim and tiny white and black satin bows down the front.

The best part was it made my boobs look a lot bigger. I put on the leather boy shorts, black and white thigh-high stockings, and the greatest boots ever: they were black, soft leather, and came to my knees. They were flat heeled with extra tread so I looked taller. If one is to get a make over, then it should be extreme.

Next, I had a thin coat that fit perfectly and flowed and waved. It was cornflower blue and matched my eyes perfectly. I slipped on black, fingerless gloves and took a deep breath, "Well?"

"You look bad ass," Dana said.

I walked out of the tent, and all stared. Oh no, I thought. Maybe I looked terrible and was still too flabby for this outfit, but no, they were all smiling and nodding with appreciation. Pax whistled. Virgil's eyes twinkled.

Danny motioned me over to a mirror. It was a big one set into a frame of polished honey-oak, and when he tilted it just so, I could see my entire self. My reflection looked shocked.

Who was this girl with the clear, fine white skin, big blue eyes, and flowing black hair? I moved a foot, and so did she, (the girl in the mirror). I raised a hand, and so did she. The warrior I saw was I!

Danny strapped knives on my thighs and added a bag to my belt.

"Are you ready Alice?"

"I am," I said, unsure if I were or not.

Each of us wore similar silver chains around our necks with iolite knotted in the strands of silver, used to travel more easily.

Danny handed me a ring made of silver, which actually was two thin bands joined by an emerald cut stone of iolite, a blue-purple stone.I slid it on my finger; it was what I was to give to the girl when we found her. Limmerfer wore a narrow collar with one stone set in silver.

"Let's do it. Umm…Danny, how do we get there?" It was only now and after weeks of training and toning my body (I lost those twenty pounds plus seven more) that I wondered how we were supposed to get to hell. It's not something you commonly think about or want to do, right?

Danny grinned and motioned us to follow him. There was a small hole under a willow tree, like a rabbit's hole, only bigger. "This is how we go. Take a leap." With a snappy salute, Danny hopped right into the hole and vanished; the cat was right behind.

I shrugged and followed, and my friends joined me.

Just like that, we were off to hell.

Chapter Eight: Down the Rabbit Hole to Hell

I fell for a long time. What? You didn't think hell was *down?* I fell for so long that I got sleepy and wondered if I would go right through the world and pop out in Australia or somewhere like that. I had no idea what they ate in Australia, but I was getting hungry, and I might find some really strange food when I landed.

I worried for my mother and father and wondered if they would miss me, even if Danny had explained that time wouldn't be the same for me as it was for up there. But anyway, besides the *time* issues and the food, I worried if my coat was wrinkled or what hell was going to be like.

Dana and I talked a while as we fell.

"I wonder how long we will fall?" Dana asked, "it's not bad since we're going slowly, and it's calming. It is very curious, though."

"No clue. What is vegemite? Do they eat it in Australia? I wonder if that's what we'll eat there."

Dana shrugged, "I think it's a fungus. They like bar-be-cues, so maybe we'll find decent food, but why are you worried about Australia?"

"I keep thinking we'll fall all the way through and come out on the other side of the world," I laughed, "I guess that's impossible but so is everything else in my life right now." It was unlike me to worry about food or Australia or to show curiosity about falling.

"This is unreal, isn't it? I keep thinking we are in a dream."

"I know," I said, "it makes no sense and feels unreal, but I know I have worked my butt off for weeks. I think I'm kind of nervous and scared of what we'll find in hell."

"I know. Monsters. And Danny said dinosaurs. Weird. I don't want to be eaten by a T-Rex or anything."

"We'll watch out for them. Danny seems to know his business even if half the time he acts like a rabbit."

"He does. Strange. Virgil likes you."

"Don't go there…not interested…just wanna get this done, save the world, and go back to normal. I like normal."

Finally, our fall slowed, and there was a bottom; we landed softly. Corey fell down because he wasn't expecting the trip down to end but got up again, brushing himself off, "Did you feel like we would fall forever?" he asked, "that was fantastic. Did you see all the stuff as we fell? I watched a half a dozen movies, I think."

"I didn't see movies," I said, "I just rested a lot."

Coral nodded, "I slept good." He stretched and yawned. He did look well rested. Dark circles had vanished from beneath his eyes.

There was a room before us. We went in.

We looked around the hallway and saw a few dusty chairs, a table, a door, and lights, besides cupboards along the walls.

Danny carried a few bags, and from one, he removed bottles of water and sandwiches of roast beef. I knew Coral made them because in the aluminum foil were garlic-dill pickles, and in a last baggie was a sour apple.

We ate every crumb.

A small zipped pouch contained a meal for the cat, and he ate his, then sat, and washed himself.

Danny encouraged us to use the restroom behind the door. It was more of an outhouse as the bottom of the toilet was a dark hole. I heard squeaking below and imagined rats.

I had a fear of falling in or dropping something into the pit. After I washed my hands, I walked back to where we gathered.

A window was near the door, and I went over to peep out. The glass was smudged with some haze, so I tried to rub it away but only smeared it more. Luckily, I had a tissue and cleaned off an area so I could see outside.

I don't know what I expected, but first view of hell was a shocking view.

Chapter Nine: First Sights of Hell

I saw a narrow street outside where people walked. Some of them looked normal, but others had horns, lizard tails, or monstrous features, all monsters from the worst nightmares.

I saw concrete and steel beams, everything in grey and shades of grey. Angles. Sharp angles filled the street, making the buildings look cold and impersonal.

They were industrial looking without plants, yards, or anything that might make them look welcoming. Between buildings, monster-looking vendors ran stalls and sold things I couldn't imagine, nor did I want to.

Alongside the streets were deep canals filled with something I couldn't quite make out and ugly steel bridges crossing the canals so the people could get from the middle of the road to the doorways of the buildings or houses.

Two females caught my eye. They wore red, very short shorts and seven-inch platform heeled shoes. When the females turned to the side, I saw breasts the size and firmness of honey dew melons, tightly packed into black leather halters. One had a head full of flowing red hair, and the other had white-blonde hair, cut super short and styled like a boy.

Danny looked out from the side.

"Prostitutes?" I asked.

"Yes. Female ones. Lice-hookers."

"Huh?"

Danny nodded, "They are gorgeous in body and face, and few men can resist them. They're expensive, as well. But when a man buys one and tries to enjoy himself, lice by the billions flow from the skin, popping out all over, and the lice swarm the victim."

"That's horrible," I said.

"They were not careful before and didn't think about the criminal element they were spreading, and now they are tormented by lice. Poetic justice is key here."

"And what happens to them? The men?" I asked.

"The lice run up their noses and down their throats, and they suffocate in a terrible way. The lice feed on them, too. Then, the men die, but this is hell, as you know, so the poor sods come back to life afterwards.

Most will grab another lice-hooker right away even though the men have suffered. They are suffocated and eaten alive by their own lust, so to speak."

"Why do they do it, knowing that?"

"It's hell. Forever.A miserable suffocation and lice creepy crawling; it's better than the same thing every day, same misery, same unhappiness. It's a new torture, and that's worth something."

I didn't agree, but that was my own belief. As I watched, both women were bought, and they vanished across a bridge and into an alley with the men. I was glad I didn't have to see the billions of lice emerge.

"That's disgusting," I said,

"Sadly, that's one of the less horrible things you will see here. Sex trade is very popular here and even greatly encouraged."

Since my eyes had adjusted, I could see more of the canals now. They carried sludgy, filthy water filled with nasty debris and bones.

Danny whispered that was sewer and that bones were common to see in the sludge. The toilet we used flowed into the open sewer.

"There is a shop there that can give you a few minutes respite from torture, but the price is a treasured memory, and you lose it. You will find some down here who remember very little, only enough to keep their punishments keen, but they have traded away everything that might have given them any balm."

Danny motioned to show us a small vial of something he was holding. "You need to use this powder. Snort it." Danny pulled the small vial from his pocket, showed it to us, and set it on the table. He treated it as if it were delicate and expensively rare.

"Coke?" Corey asked, a little excited.

Danny shook his head, "No. It's very, very valuable down here. It's made of one-eyed demon bones, and those are hard to find.

You are carrying many gemstones now, but the little bit of powdered, one-eyed demon bones I procured is worth a hundred times your gems. It is horribly costly. I umm...paid a lot for it," Danny unconsciously touched his eye patch.

"Danny, tell me you didn't...." My knees felt watery with the thought of his trading an eye for the powder. How painful that would be both physically and emotionally.

"An eye is worth a lot, Alice. I traded it for the powder. I had to. All of you need to sniff a pinch; it will dull your sense of smell so that instead of all the foul stenches, you'll get just a bit of them."

I was wordless over the fact that he had given his own eye to procure the powder for our comfort and to ensure we did the best we could. It was a terrible sacrifice.

Dana asked, "Why do we need it?" She inquisitively looked at the powder, ready to do as Danny asked.

"Because the smell alone down here drives most people insane for hundreds or thousands of years, the *important, wealthy* people have the powder so they don't suffer the reek."

"Umm. They could just stop having open sewers and clean up? Then, no one would need the stuff," Pax said. He sniffed the white powder and said he didn't feel a thing, "They could bathe and do common sense things."

"You'd get a tax for not littering. Contributions to the *State of Decay* are very serious things here. People can be arrested and tortured for not using the sewer system enough," Danny said. "*The State of Decay* is very important, and everyone shows public support. If you vomit into the street, you are likely to get applause."

I looked at the canals and shivered. Yuk.

The sky was reddish grey and polluted, probably just how they liked it here. On the table, I saw a bottle with a little tag.

Drink me.

I looked to Danny. I poured the wine into the glasses I found in a cupboard, not clean ones, but dusty ones that fit right in with the other dust and dirt. Sniffing powder and drinking unknown wine, it was a wild time.

Danny said the wine would mask our auras so that people wouldn't easily be able to see that we were alive and not supposed to be in hell. The entire *dead* and *alive* thing was very confusing to me. People here were dead in our world and alive here. My friends and I were alive both places.

"The story we will use is that you are new here in hell, so you can get by with reacting in horrified ways as you begin to understand the misery here. We will say I am your guide.

Some may try to frighten or disgust you because they score points for that. Some may be very pitiful, but don't let your sympathy go too far as they can't be helped at all." Danny pulled on white gloves that hid his strange fingers.

He spoke and looked different now, and I wondered why he was in disguise down here. It was a question and some random thoughts I had that I filed away for later.

CHapter TeN: I AM NeW Here iN HeLL

Walking out of that room into the street was one of the most difficult things we had ever done. All of us looked at one another with dread as we stepped out. Faintly, I could smell rot, smoke, and other scents that I couldn't quite place, but they were fleeting anyway.

Walking over the bridge, I willed myself not to look at the sludge. Into a canal, Danny poured out a bag of rodents' skeletons, some with their scaly tails still fresh. He said it was for the owners of the house and to keep them from being taxed for not contributing to the *State of Decay*.

I didn't ask who owned the house.

The cobblestones were black and set with concrete all around them, but Danny told us that the stones were made in factories that belched out the black smoke. The lowest class of the people worked at the factories.

"And they make the stone?" I asked.

"Oh, no, Not at all. Those who *make* the stones are a step higher. The lowest class is drained of blood several times a day, and they die, and then they come back, and they are drained again.

Their blood is to help form the stones. It's really an unappreciated job. Envision being on a rigid table with a needle inserted into your vein. In a few minutes, your blood runs out a tube and into a fissure in the floor. Down below, they process your blood to make the stones. In time, you die. In a few moments, you awaken, alive again, and the blood runs out a second time. A third time. All day long for twelve hours."

"Who is the low class? How did they get to be so low here?" Pax asked.

"People trying to sell their souls for power and money when they were alive are automatically regulated to the low strata when they die. They expect to have everything they want but are tricked.

BBDU is a master of lies. The low people are somewhat like mosquitoes, little people that aggravate with big aspirations. They aren't evil enough for a big, important position here, but trust me, there are millions of them, silly little wannabes."

"I guess if people knew what would happen, they wouldn't try to sell their souls," Annie said. "That's horrible."

"In the factories, some people have bone taken from them. Humans or demons either are fine. They cut off the legs and arms, and then the workers chop up the body and remove the bones.

The grout work between the stones is dust and bone, and that is what the workers want the bone for. When they finish flensing, the head goes on a shelf."

I used a toe of my boot to rub the grout, shivering, "And then? What happens to the heads?"

"The head might stay on the shelves, fully aware, eternally. They feel the pain of losing their corporeal bodies, of course.

When there are too many, they might be tossed out into the canal or garbage or kicked about as a ball; parts of the head might be used for other things; the eyes could be food or used in potions for magic."

People shouldn't try to bargain with their souls. I said that.

"Meh, you can't tell anyone anything. No one takes warnings seriously," Danny told us, "you should know that by now." He pointed out the way we were to go, with a caveat that we were about to face a specific hazard here in hell. We were about to have our first fight.

"Why doesn't anyone just clean them out for good?" Pax asked, looking at the bunch of hooligans awaiting us.

"Pax, Pax, Pax. It's *hell*, remember?" Dana said, "It only makes sense a bunch of bullies would be in hell."

Down the alley where we had to go, a large group of boys and girls stood around, smoking dope, drinking something red and thick, and laughing loudly. The boys were all pimply-faced, big, and dumb-looking. They hawked snot and spat globs on the walls until the walls shone with their noxious bodily fluid.

Most wore jeans that showed their butt cracks; ugly, washed-out tee shirts; and big, black, biker boots with metal riveted into the edges to match their belts. The boots looked enormous on their fat feet.

The girls were divided. Half were rough-looking, snapping gum angrily, and smoking. They had mean, piggy eyes, wide doughy faces, thin lips and were unattractive; the anger and hatred ruined any good looks they might have had. The other half of the girls were nearly the opposite: slender with curves, very pretty and were dressed in cute, flashy clothing such as skinny jeans, brightly colored blouses, and fashionable sandals. They had perfectly coiffed hair, straight and bouncy, and they texted one another constantly, giggling and exclaiming loudly.

"Bullies," Annie sniffed, "What about the pretty ones? Who are those cute girls with the bullies?"

"Mean girls," I said. I knew who they were. Those were the ones who singled out other kids in school, wrote malicious, spiteful things on their social pages, and took unflattering videos that they shared and laughed over.

In high school, a picture taken of a girl in the shower or in her underwear often went viral as the mean girls shared it. They posted criticisms of the girl's physical attributes, laughed at her in the halls, left her hateful notes, and generally made every day a living hell.

The girls harassed victims until they broke their intended target's hearts and souls. How many girls had committed suicide after being terrorized by mean girls?

"Passing through," Danny said as we walked into the alley.

"I don't think so. What's with the stupid clothes?" a pretty blonde asked. Her big eyes were blank with stupidity and mean with spite.

"I dunno. I was gonna ask why you were wearing them," Annie snapped back. She disliked those kinds of people, ones who purposely hurt others.

"You have to pay if you wanna get through here, or you are dead," a boy said. As he grinned, a fat pimple broke on his chin.

"Not paying and not putting up with bullying," Pax said.

"Then, we're gonna kick your ass. You want me to rearrange your face before we kill you?"

Pax gave us all a funny look as if he might start laughing over all this. The bullies were predictable with everything they said and did.

We wondered how much lunch money they had taken, how many lunches they had stolen or squashed, how many bloody noses they had caused, and how many kids they had made cry on school buses. For the despair they caused, they lived here in hell.

"All of these caused so many terrors and so much heartache that their victims killed themselves." Danny said.

I let my jaw drop as Danny told us that. I was angry.

Two fat boys came at Pax, and the fight was on as soon as Pax landed one of his boots in one of the boy's pudgy, soft gut.

Annie and Dana each took on two of the mean girls since those types couldn't fight with anything but their foul mouths. Corey jumped a big muscular boy, and Coral began slamming his big fists into the faces of the other scowling boys who came at him with switchblades. One flying back kick later and I was punching and dodging furiously.

My first fighting partner went down as a meaty slab of cowardice, hugging his belly and crying at being given back what he had dished so often.

I grabbed one of the baseball bats the bullies had been threatening us with and swung it as if I were a hitting a homerun. The girl, with short hair, twice my size, and yelling curses, froze like a character in a comic book when the hard wood of the bat caught her under the jaw,"You little bitch, I'm gonna…."

She didn't finish her threat. Teeth flew wildly, but I already had the bat raised and brought it down on her head. Blood poured onto the cobblestones as she fell down. The stones seemed to suck at the blood, and it soaked in quickly, making the stones glow with deep crimson.

That was interesting.

Stomping across her back, I hit the next girl in her ribs and then in the head.

"Don't like it, do you? You shouldn't have brought it," said Corey as he took the knife away from the kid he was fighting, and to my shock, whipped the blade across the other boy's throat, leaving him to bleed out. Blood sopped out beneath the boy.

I knew that they wouldn't *stay* dead because they were doomed to die, suffer, and then to do it all over again. Still, even if we were attacked first, it was hard for me to slaughter people. I didn't like killing and, of course, had not practiced that part, but now I had to do it.

Coral finished popping some heads open, and Pax stomped his boots to get the blood off. Coral looked a little sick as he surveyed the brains leaking out.

Annie and Dana smiled at one another.

"We did it," Annie smiled, "just like Coral taught us."

Dana smirked, "I knew we could, and I feel better after that payback."

"You just watched?" I asked Danny and Virgil. They leaned against a slab of cement, watching and yawning.

"You had this fight in the bag. There was no doubt. One thing, keep your arms up a little higher, Dana. One almost got in a punch. Annie, don't be afraid to kick a little harder. Coral and Pax did well. Corey, you can finish the job faster. You aren't supposed to enjoy it, or you'll end up down here forever, right? "

"What about me?"

Danny looked at me, "You were at a level three, at most. I expected more enthusiasm and ass kicking from you. That won't work when you meet some really tough characters."

"It was my first, Danny. I don't care why there are here, but I hate hurting people," I said. I was more than a little pissed off at his critique.

"They are very bad people, remember. And no matter the damage, they will be back."

"I'll try to fight harder next time," I said uninterestedly, "but it's sickening."

"Good, but still…a little more enthusiasm, please," he said. "Never enjoy it. Do it because we have a higher purpose. Once you like the blood…well…you know there will soon be room down here for more. Don't mess up. I don't want to leave any of you down here."

"Great, you dumb fuck, telling me not to *enjoy* it," Cory snapped.

"Could that happen? I mean…we could get left?" Pax asked.

"It's a possibility. But we have to go. We *can't be late*." Danny looked at his pocket watch, put it back into his pocket, and kind of hopped a little down the alley.

Chapter Eleven: Pond of Tears and Horde of Rats

A woman slipped from the shadows. She was dressed oddly, even for hell, in a slip of a dress that showed one bare breast. She stood tall and strong and had a determined look on her face. I asked who she was as she ran past.

"Penthesilea, Amazon Queen. Maybe you recall her story. She fought for the Trojan side and did amazingly well, but she fell, and then Achilles raped her as she lay dying. He's a piss ant by the way and lives here for his cruelty and sinful ways," Virgil said. "She could have beaten the bullies, but there were too many of them; she took the chance to get by after you did your job. Smart of her."

"Smart? Letting us do the work? Can't she fight?" I fumed.

"Sure she can and will, but she didn't want to face them all alone. She is a far better warrior than you are, but she chose to be clever, instead."

"I think she was cheap in letting us do the work," I complained.

We walked out into what, back home, would be called a commons or a park. There were statues, and I recognized Adolph Hitler, a chubby former US President, and a Hollywood movie starlet carved from the smooth stone. I bet you can guess those two, I mean. Benches had tiny nails lining the seats, and when I saw that some people were sitting on benches, I had goose bumps. Blood seeped between the slats to the cobblestones as the nails punctured the flesh of their buttocks.

Grass was more of a spongy green fungus, the trees were gnarled, bare, and dying, and the water from the fountain was spurting in jumps and starts as if pumping from an artery, smelling like cat piss. Next to it and along the edges of the fountain on stone sides, sat misshapen women, or females, I should say, who reached out talon-tipped fingers to catch drops of the yellow liquid and lick them away.

Terrible tumors and growths covered their faces, and their bodies were jointed in odd places but very curvaceous with wide, generous hips, big firm bosoms, and shapely legs. Their skin was smooth, creamy greenish, and disgusting. What the tumors didn't cover looked human-life except for their eyes, which were bloodshot in shades of pink, red, and reddish brown.

The spawn of these beings scampered lizard-like through the park and resembled their mothers.

"These are mainly the demon wives of some of the higher-ups. They spend their time here in the park or shopping," Virgil said.

"There is the *Pond of Tears*." We looked at the water. Virgil explained that all the tears people shed for their loved ones in hell landed here. It looked like the most pleasant part of hell, a clear pond of salt water, a shore of sand.

"It's not as bad here. Tears are okay, I guess," Coral said thoughtfully.

Danny snickered, "Tears. And the sand, yellow and fine? That is made of eye boogers and the crust eyes can get. You can imagine how repulsive it is to be caught way over there in the *Swamp of Conjunctivitis* or pink eye if you are local. It's toxic, and any contact leads to ghastly eye infections."

"Yuk," Dana said. She looked at me with disgust, wondering how Danny could snicker. I didn't know how he could, either.

Some boats sailed far away. Danny and Virgil urged us to hurry along.

"Here. Stand over here," Danny said, "we are about to see another rough part of this area."

In the distance, I saw a smudge, but it was closer each time I looked. The demon children played in the sand, not aware of the black mass approaching.

We saw that the black mass was a horde of rats running towards us at a ferocious speed, eyes beady, noses twitching, tails slinking. I moved closer to Coral who sat a strong arm about my shoulders.

Virgil took over, pulling me close to him, and Coral let go. When Limmerfer meowed pitifully, I reached down and gathered him into my arms to stroke his ears. He climbed up until he was against my heartbeat, facing away from the threat.

I felt a little dizzy and warm next to Virgil as he held me against his hard muscled body. He was safe to be close to, but he also felt a little dizziness. I tried to not think about it; he was only protecting me.

Rats poured onto the beach of sand and raced to the children. The rats' fur writhed with fleas and shone with grease. The first rats leaped at a child, hooking yellowed incisors onto his small body and scrambled up to nip at his timorous, waxy green face.

More rats climbed the other children as if they were trees, using razor sharp claws to hold on. Everywhere were squeals and shrieks of pain; demon mothers ran to their children, yelling for help as their children were attacked.

I almost reeled with horror. Vigil held me tighter so I didn't fall as my legs went to jelly. I wanted to hide my face against his shoulder but watched, remembering this was where I had to work for a while.

The sound was like pulling duct tape off a roll as the rats ripped away strips and strands of skin from faces and bodies. The pieces looked rather like long pieces of wilted, pale lettuce with red gore splashed about. Bits of clothing fell like confetti, along the droplets of blood that festooned the sand. More screams.

The rats became slick with the blood from their victims but continued to bite and eat the demon flesh until we saw white bone flashing in the frenzied attack.

Bare finger bones and arm bones waved at the sky for help as the children screamed with pain and fear.

In a while, only bones, the confetti, bits of flesh, and globs of red and yellow, fatty slime remained on the beach. The rats, following some leader, dove into the salty pond and swam as a thick, dark unit back across to another beach, sated with their meal. Little movement was left on the sand as they fled to the infectious swamp.

"In a while, the children and mothers will reincorporate, and we again will see the mothers sitting on the benches and the demonic children playing in the park and coming out to the sand if we stayed.

This attack happens every day at the same time, and each time, they have forgotten the terror and pain of the rats. It's not pleasant, and it's best to stay away so you aren't bitten as well," Danny told us.

"It's terrible here," I said. It was terrible when Virgil let me go, too.

Some of the rats remained, still chewing at the flesh. I went over and kicked one as hard as I could, and it squealed as it went flying through the air. Cory and Dana each kicked one, and Coral snapped one under his boot, "I don't like no rats," he said.

I liked the crunch as I kicked another away. I posed for a second in my badass outfit, my feet spread a little, and hands in fists by my sides. I felt more like a warrior each passing minute.

Limmerfer sniffed at the rats but didn't touch them other than to bat them away with sharp-clawed paws.

Chapter Twelve: Open Markets

We followed Danny and Virgil around the pond and into a new quarter. Danny said it was nearing dinnertime and we should try not to be appalled, warning us that this was going to be awful. *Dinnertime* would no doubt be miserable in this place.

At the open market, they sold vile things although Danny said this was considered a classy area in which to shop for food. A gnarled, old woman called out to us to see her wares. "Fresh, sweet meats," she said, pointing out a tray of penises lined up like sausages and testicles with a slice on onion on top and braised with butter. I almost didn't know what they were in this odd context and because they were so white, drained of blood and flabby.

Another was a penis smothered with maggots and a plate of pale things that at first I thought were funny-colored fried eggs but were breasts, nipples pink and purple and set into a dish such as fried eggs with penises as sausages in a macabre breakfast offering. In another dish were more personal female parts, pickled.

"Where do they come from?" Cory asked.

" Maybe adulterers or maybe Flense Banks. The poor people go there and offer body parts for a few pennies so they can afford food or things they need," Danny explained. "A man might go in and give his privates, which are worth more than some parts. Toes and fingers are purchased for use in bars such *as* Hot Digits with sauce. Some banks buy buttocks for the *barby* and others buy tongues to pickle."

Annie gagged.

Pax looked puzzled, "They walk around with privates cut away?"

"Sure. You see women without breasts, or they wear socks wadded up, and the men can't...yanno, and it never heals...always an open wound, so it hurts like a bitch, but what can they do? It's hell," Danny said.

The old woman offered us a kidney pie, and I shuddered, "Marinated in its own piss," she called.

Hellfire Sweets offered familiar shapes covered in a thin coating of chocolate.

"I'd like to buy *BBDU* and burn this place to the ground. It should be destroyed," I said, "Everything and everyone here should be cast into nothingness. There is no reason for all this. It's a total...bother."

Virgil nodded, "I agree. But Lucifer was an ass and caused trouble, and so this place was formed. It's all his doing...selfish prick...he formed the negative space."

In the next stall were breasts, decorated with dried herbs and the owner of the stall assured us they had been well cooked on a brimstone grill. He praised brimstone and brimstone accessories.

Pax gripped my hand as we passed a place that had strips of cured flesh hanging from wires and fishhooks above. "We got demon jerky, human jerky, hybrid jerky. I got pork belly, man belly, demon belly...fried, braised, dried, roasted, grilled, and broiled," the owner of the booth said, "Filet-*men*-yon."

The worst part was it all smelled like bacon and made our mouths water. I turned away to avoid seeing what was roasted whole and had an apple in its mouth. I had a feeling I knew.

There were stalls with herbs, bottles of potions, more roasts that hung from the rafters of stalls, human-looking torsos, breads, vegetables, and stones, papers, and dark-colored cloth. I saw jars of pickled tongues and thought of Coral's dill pickles.

Danny looked over the vegetables with Coral and selected some: fruit, bread, and a block of goat's cheese. I didn't think any of us would be able to eat the items Danny wrapped and put into his bag.

A woman waved a hand over her pots, "Ready to eat:prostate pudding, demon food cake, caramel ears, and joint jelly. It's all to die for," she giggled. I was shocked that her body was turned backwards, and she had to use her hands without seeing. I asked why her head was on backwards.

"Fortune teller. She lied about being one and took money for lies, so since she couldn't see the future, she is doomed to look behind her here in hell," Virgil said, "It's strange, isn't it?"

"Creepy," I told him.

"We'll see more of them later as we descend. There's an entire place where they twist the heads that way."

I saw an immense, muscular demon in the next booth. He was greenish yellow and had nubs of horns on his forehead, a bull-looking face with a wide set nose, and the body of a man. An enormous bulge wiggled under his loin cloth as he looked me over.

Hornets buzzed his face, and one stung him. He winced with the pain but still stared at me. I figured that over the eons, he was stung a lot, and although it hurt, it was familiar.

I ignored the wiggling of his privates, "What do you sell?"

When he grinned, dirty, brown, square teeth showed, "I have three bred humans."

"What is that? I'm new here."

"I know. I smell your newness." He sniffed towards me, obscenely. He explained in loving detail that in hell, demons could have children with demons, female humans with male humans, and humans with demons. The offspring had no souls and were empty vessels.

"I have the offspring of humans for sale. You can find such all along here, and some are for eating, some are for playthings, and some are for servants. Your stall dealer tells you what he has trained or procured his wares for."

"Oh," I said, "and what are your three humans for?" I felt my face turn numb with the absurdity of this conversation.

He chuckled as he pulled back a small black curtain to reveal a little platform where he had three humans chained. Each was a child of about three or four and were grossly overweight, so thick and plump that they couldn't stand but had to sit with the others in a puddle of rolls of dirty, foul-smelling flesh. I thought about chubby grub worms. I hated that I was already catching on to the way things worked here.

"Roasts," I said.

He winked, slapping at a hornet that stung his cheek.

Virgil whispered, "He is self indulgent. He was probably a sexual predator or traded in human flesh. This is his punishment: to be stung by his conscience to remind him of his selfishness. I don't think he suffers much."

As we walked away, the hornets gathered and swarmed the man to sting; it made me feel a little better as the man broke down and howled as a dozen of the tiny beasties sank their stingers into his flesh, the poison dripping in yellow tears. He howled.

CHapter THirteeN: SHe WaS a WOrM....

Danny led us down an alley to a house built of old wood and concrete blocks, another dirty, dusty house. We walked across the bridge, as beneath us, sludge carried small bones along the canal. We reached the opened door, and we ducked inside. I had to let my eyes adjust to the dim candlelight of the house.

The woman before us was A. Monster. I. Think.

This was almost beyond what I could deal with. She stood very tall, about seven feet; she was a few inches taller than Coral. Several rows of small arms stuck out of her body that was not so much a torso but rolls of fat, which made her seem to be segmented. Her legs looked merged, and she was shaped exactly like a caterpillar.

She had soft, mushy-looking flesh and a row of flat breasts, five in all. She wasn't concerned that we saw her in a nude state, but then maybe worms didn't care.

Her face was a wide, sloppy-lipped mouth with stubs of tiny teeth, a flat nose, big golden eyes, and antennae that swept up and away from her face majestically. Despite everything I have said, she seemed almost regal and very motherly.

It was rude, but we all stared at this…this…I didn't have a word for her.

Virgil introduced us, "This is Cassie."

"I'm sorry I'm staring. I haven't been here long, and I am not used to people and places yet. I find you very unusual and foreign to me."

That was the best I could say to explain why we all looked at her.She was a worm.I was attempting to be as polite as possible because I knew she was hiding us in her home at great danger to herself.

Cassie smiled, which was not a pretty response, "It's okay, dear. I know we take some getting used to. I looked like any of you when I was alive as I was a pretty young girl before I died of the plague. I was the prettiest, youngest nun in the convent.Then, I descended into this place, but now, well, you see what I look like. I have changed." Her eyes blinked.

"Why?" Coral asked, "why are you different now? I mean, if I may be so personal and ask. I apologize if I am out of line."

"Those of us who were nuns, priests, rabbis, imams, and monks who got in trouble were changed once we got here. We became monstrous." She twittered as she moved that huge body to another room, motioning with her many hands for us to follow. Her kitchen was small. Coral got busy with the food Danny had collected.

"I forget that people are shocked to see what I am. For hundreds of years, I cried, but did that change anything? Not a bit. Now, I accept what I look like."

I wondered what she had done to be sent here.

She was a worm and how weird was that?

As if she could read my mind, she said, "I was that pretty young nun, and I stole coins from the church. I had a streak of vanity, you see since I was so pretty, and those coins bought cosmetics that I wore in secret. I was a thief, vain, and a hypocrite to the church," Cassie said.

"That isn't...I mean, there are worse crimes you could have committed. This seems a little harsh," Dana muttered sympathetically.

Virgil replied, "A worm in the grain ruins the entire barrel, just like a worm in an apple ruins the fruit. She was considered to be the worm that was ruining the church."

"I would be punished for saying so, but *BBDU* enjoys transforming us as an affront to Him. Failures of the churches and religion are enjoyable here," Cassie sighed a little. But then she picked up our cat and cooed to him, causing him to purr happily.

Once Cassie was sure Coral and Dana had everything they needed to make a consumable dinner, she and I went to her window to look out. I saw a few hookers again, two humans and one demoness, dressed in short skirts over long, sexy legs that ended in strappy sandals with platform heels. Both humans had three breasts each in tight halters, and the demoness had one breast in the middle of her chest.

I decided that hell did a thriving sex business. Cassie explained that once a month, prostitutes went to a clinic to be infected with syphilis, gonorrhea, and HIV. *Medical Act of 1982* requires all prostitutes to '*share the burn*'."

"Everything is backwards here," I said, "but I as a warrior when in my real life, I am a boring, plain person, is backwards as well."

Chapter Fourteen: No Slate to Make Marks On

A fat man came towards us, a leash in his hands. On chains about their necks were three small children: a fat one who would be roasted, a thin one who might be a servant, and cute little girl with freckles and sad eyes. It did no good, but the children fiddled with their collars, hoping to loosen them as the leather eternally chafed their skin. The tiny girl tripped on a cobblestone and fell, skinning her knee.

Kicking and cursing, the fat man began kicking her violently. The three hookers joined and began kicking her as well, laughing. They kicked all the children. Their sharp spiked heels bruised the little ones who screamed with pain.

The hookers were Lice-Hookers because I saw the wave of tiny bug-creatures lunge for the man who got too close to them as he yanked at the children. The lice might jump onto the children, too.

Cory and Annie watched out another window and looked at me with dismay. It was hard to watch the brutality.

I spun, grabbed Cory and Annie, and bolted for a back door Cory had found. Running, I didn't feel tired but instead, energy flowed through my body as I played out the image, in my mind, of the violent people kicking the children.

We sprinted down a dirty, needle-filled alley (a waste since Danny had said throwing used needles into the canal was encouraged) and around the corner so we could approach the people in the street without giving away where we were staying.

"Hey, get away from her and stop kicking her." I waved a pipe I found and pretended it was a sword. I decided right then, I wanted a sword for battles. Guns were a last resort as they attracted too much attention, so we didn't have them.

"Mind your own business, bitch," the plump man snarled. He yanked at his '*roast*' brutally. "Get up."

"You stop kicking, too," I ordered one of the hookers.

"'*Ho,* you wanna mix it up with Lee'noleum? Huh?'"

"Linoleum?Unreal," I said. She moved into my personal space, ready for hair pulling and fingernail raking, but that's not how I fought.

Lee'noleum raised a hand to grab my hair, and the fight was on. I took her arm and swung her around so I could pin her arm, painfully, way up high on her back. I jerked at her arm to make her screech. I kneed her in her big butt, causing her to fall on her knees. Barely catching herself with one hand, she almost did a face-plant on the ground and scraped both knees as she went down.

She didn't like someone her own size fighting back.

Carrying through, I pushed her down and planted a boot on her back. Rearing back, I popped her head with my pipe, splitting her skull. It's not as if she would stay dead, but she would remember the headache I gave her. I hit her until blood and brains leaked.

Cory took on the other two hookers, and we found out that when the hookers "die", the lice become free to feast fully. He broke both of the hookers' necks with quick snaps. When they came back, they would suffer a world of pain as well.

Annie jumped the fat man and took away his big machete. Coral taught us well how to disarm and fight, and Annie put the lessons into practice. Annie disarmed the fat man. *Literally.* His arms went flying. Annie, quite and sweet, chopped off his arms, and blood spurted everywhere as he ran around wailing.

We stopped the fight to watch him. I ducked as a spray of sticky red blood flew at me. It missed and went onto the road. He ran away, crying and blubbering with snot running down his face.

The '*roast*' looked at us stupidly, not understanding we had set them free.

"Go on and go somewhere safe. You're free," I told the thin girl.

She nodded a little, looking at the dead hookers. The lice, with tiny popping sounds, were eating the demoness; they had finished her greenish skin and were to the bloody layer underneath with no signs of being finished.

The thin girl and fat child waddled and walked away down the street, without looking back at us. I had the feeling that they had no clear concept of what had occurred. We turned to go back down the street and around to the back door, but as we turned the corner, we saw that the small girl with freckles was following us quietly.

She was like a stray cat.

"Shoo...go on now," Cory tried waving her away.

The child made a faint hissing noise but didn't retreat.

Annie shook her head, "No, she's adorable. We can feed her."

"She isn't a cat, Annie. You wanna feed and water her and take her for walks and clean up after her? She's...well...not a real human."

"Cory, that's horrible," Annie said, tears filling her eyes.

"We'll keep her a while," I said, making Annie smile. Cory gave me a partial hug before we went inside.

"We saw," Coral said, his voice like deep thunder, rolling and booming, "You went out there to fight for no reason and could have gotten caught or worse."

"I couldn't watch that fat slob do that shit," Cory said. His face lost the angry look and lit up as he saw Cassie's hookah, "Awe, man, this is cool. Cassie, you rock."

I shrugged. Cory was like a child with wavering moods.

Danny looked the stray over, "She's not hurt, and she's a cute kid. The thing is she was born here of two humans and is without a *soul*."

"What's that *mean*?" I asked.

"Well, she couldn't go to Heaven, and she couldn't go to your world. She's here forever."

"So are the rest, right?"

"True. She never had a choice and never lived outside of here. She'll never know of the other world. She is neither good not evil, but without a soul...no slate to make marks on."

I washed her face and hands for her, then braided her hair French style, and tied it off with a bright blue ribbon Cassie gave me. The child didn't know her name and spoke very quietly in whispers if she spoke at all. She was afraid of the men. "I want to name her Dinah. Is that okay? Do you want to be Dinah?"

She smiled and hugged me. I told her we would eat soon, and Cassie gave us some scraps of cloth and some odds and ends that we made a doll with. It wasn't a great dolly, but it was something she could have of her very own for once. Coral watched with interest.

Danny huffed and sighed. I ignored him.

Virgil watched me.

Coral made spaghetti with sauce and bread with pesto dipping oil; also, we had a fruit salad for dessert. Dinah ate as if she were starved, which Danny said she probably was. We were hungry and had seconds and thirds of the food.

Dinah finished eating and sat on the floor to pat Limmerfer's fur as he purred happily. Dinah waggled a string, and Limmy chased it, but we saw the set of his jaw and knew he did it to please her, not because he enjoyed the chase. Lim ran, did a few flips, slid along the floor, jumped, and made Dinah giggle with his antics.

Chapter Fifteen: Parade of Lamma, Hashish, and a Cat

"Tomorrow morning the Parade of Lammas will be going down the street out there. Of course, it runs all day as there are so many streets to cover," Cassie told us.

"Lammas?"

"People celebrate it back home differently; you'd never notice it as anything, but here, they follow the old Druid holidays because it is so associated with paganism. It's kind of a laugh at those who think pagan holidays have anything to do with hell, see? An inside joke. Lammas was always the celebration of harvest, especially wheat," Danny told us.

"What would hell do with wheat?" Pax laughed.

"Inside joke, remember. Usually they have a float with big glass jars with wheat inside: people suffocating in wheat and people with wheat stalks stuffed…well, you can imagine, giant wheat-people loaves of bread. Other entertainment were the demonic band, playing humans as the instruments such as strumming ribs, and drumming fat bellies, and you don't want to know how the horn section works. Obese acrobats with multiple arms and legs perform along the way, horses…skeletal ones with demon riders, and midget clowns…anything you can imagine but with twists you wouldn't like," Cassie finished.

"Maybe we can sleep through that," Cory suggested, "it sounds like a depressing parade."

Cassie nodded, "I'll share some ear plugs with you. It is very depressing."

Danny told me he wanted to show me some things around hell, and we would go as a small group. Cory wanted to stay and smoke hashish with Cassie, and Annie wanted to stay with Dinah and watch her play with Limmerfer. Dana and Pax went with us.

CHapter Sixteen: Satan's Tit

The bar was called Satan's Tit. That was a stupid name I thought, but then who was I to think up names of bars in hell?

Danny ordered for us: an imported beer so we wouldn't have to drink the local swill, and we found a place to watch everyone from a back booth where the din was slightly less than eardrum piercing. The music was rap music, so yes, it was indeed hell there.

Our waitress, with yellow skin, was a demoness, wearing a halter for four breasts and a short denim skirt. From under the skirt, thin, shining tentacles wriggled from underneath like a petticoat with fringe, making me shiver with disgust. Her nostrils were held wide-open by metal rings so we could see right into her sinus cavities if we had so wanted. Instead of ears, she had metal disks covering the sides of her head with holes for hearing. We could see them plainly, as her orange hair was shorn very short and spiky.

Danny told us, "The ear covers were popular fashion. They remove their ears, sell them, and cover the spot with those plates. The nose rings are all the rage, as well. She's in high fashion."

A human at the bar sported slash marks across his face that scarred him badly. Danny said the human was a victim of a velociraptor and said we could always tell by the slashes and missing forearms; they liked to bite those off. I didn't understand why dinosaurs went to hell and asked, but Danny shrugged and said he didn't know either, really. He did know that very few dogs and only about half the cat population ended up in hell.

It seemed some cats were just evil creatures, but I never knew that before. I wondered why they would be, but I didn't ask Danny because I didn't want to think about evil cats. Limmerfer didn't seem evil, and Danny said that Limmy was actually a very good cat and was on the mission to clear his slate.

That seemed a little far-fetched.

In the bar, I saw humans and demons, and both were missing body parts, or they had strange fashions, or they were monstrous since some had crab-like pinchers, spider eyes, deformed features, matted fur, or horns. Very few looked as normal as we did, but we didn't get attention.

Danny told us, "Sorry, but you and Dana are like the homely girls here. They're ignoring you. Remember, beauty is not beauty here. Now, if you were deformed...."

"I get it," I said.

"You two are the ugly girls here," Danny went on.

"Yes, we get it," I repeated.

"The hookers here are a lower class than the lice-hookers," Danny said.

Dana gaped, "How can they be lower? No, never mind, don't tell me."

We saw that the bartender made sure to serve underage patrons doubles, and he made sure everyone drank until he tossed everything back up. Drugs were set out in little bowls such as peanuts might be in regular bars.

Danny told us that if we could smell the bar, we'd be heaving, which would be fine as everyone was encouraged to vomit on the floor. "After hours, the mess is mopped *into* the wooden floor, not mopped away."

Dana made a face and said, "Yuk, okay, hell can be bad, but it is just nasty if you ask me."

"Perversions and nastiness. Pain and misery. Sickness is highly prized. This is more involved than I would have imagined," Pax told us, "but that is what is worse for the majority, so those things are enjoyed here. Now for me, the bad thing would be no football."

"There is a sort of football, but it involves rape and bone saws, and I doubt you'd want to watch it, Pax. There is basketball, too, but that is played with dental tools, and fouls are penalized in a most painful manner. Tooth nerves are excellent to poke in for penalties." Danny clandestinely pointed out a demon with two heads, "He's a funny one. One head controls the top of his body, and the second controls the bottom part. He is funny to watch."

That was our lesson on how backwards and how terrible things could be as if we didn't know. Danny concluded, "You can't whip everyone in hell, Alice. Dinah can't be helped since she lives here. You aren't here to save the world; well, you are, but not by attacking everyone who is doing something vile."

"Then you picked the wrong person. I can't watch people harm animals or children and not help them, Danny, so just understand who I am," as I said that, it occurred to me that weeks before, I would have walked away from confrontation and would have ignored wrongdoing in order to stay uninvolved.

I guess *who I was* had changed some, right? Yep, it dawned on me then as well, and Virgil and Danny almost smiled, so they realized it as well.

CHapter SeVeNteeN: INto tHe Pot:MUSHrOoMS, DreaMS, CaterpiLLar

When we got back to Cassie's house, Annie and Coral were laughing at Cory who lay on the floor giggling, "Hey, Pax; hey, Dana; hey, Alice and Danny. Did you have fun?"

"Sure, what's up here?"

Cory giggled, "Alice, I grew really big, and my head went up high into the trees."

"Wow. Do tell?"

He nodded, "I saw this bird and scared him, and he was calling me a serpent even if I'm not green or scaled. How cool is that?"

"Very cool, Cory."

"So this bird was accusing me of wanting her eggs, but I don't eat raw eggs. Coral makes them for me over easy, but she said I had a long neck. Then, I was itty bitty, and that sucked 'cause I could have run into one of those lice, and it would be big and chase me. Scary, huh?" he kept talking.

"Really scary. Big louse after you," said Pax as he agreed.

Mesmerizing us with his story he said, "The big louse had segmented parts that overlapped like armor, and his bottom legs were pinchers like you see on a crab. That's how they hold on to your hair with those pinchers.

Up front, they have normal bug legs and can point at you when they talk, see? So the louse winked at me and said he was too big to get in my hair."

"What's wrong with Cory? Why did he see a giant louse? Did he go outside and see demons?" Dana asked.

Coral shook his head, "Nah. He and Cassie ate mushrooms of a type that I don't cook." He watched with us, and when Cory fell asleep with his mouth wide open, Coral sighed, bent down, and dragged Cory to a pallet to sleep.

Dana, Annie, and I found places on the sofa and in chairs, allowing Dinah to sleep close to Cassie. We liked Cassie a lot but sleeping next to a big caterpillar was odd to us, but not to Dinah. I feared being squashed which was weird since in my world, caterpillars worried about being squashed by *us*.

Exhausted, we slept heavily that night, and the earplugs worked well, so we slept late; Coral, Pax, and Annie were the only ones who got up to watch the Infernal Parade of Lammas and said it was as weird as anything Cory could have made up in the 'shroom-induced dreams he had. He disagreed, saying he had seen things far stranger than what we had seen so far in hell and then said Cassie had amazing hallucinogenic drugs.

When we were ready to go, Cassie walked to the door with us. I paused, wondering how we could possibly thank her enough for her help. What could I say? That I was going back home and so sorry she had to stay in hell? Not cool. To my shock, she told me she wasn't finished, "I'll go along in case you need help. Besides, I can take care of Dinah for you."

That was something we hadn't talked about. What would we do with Dinah now that we had rescued her from her handler? But the idea of taking a big worm and a little girl along on our trip was daunting. Danny frowned a little.

"Cassie, if you were harmed because of my mission, I would be heartbroken," I told her honestly. I really liked her. She was a very nice…ummm…worm.

"Silly. I will be fine. If I can help a little, then I shall," she said.

So that was how our group enlarged. We were two girls and two guys all in leathers, a girl (me) in a bustier and bright blue coat, a cute cat, a huge black man (who was forty/elderly), a guy with funny fingers and hands, a caterpillar, and a little girl.

Of course, we didn't look out of place in hell.

CHapter EighteeN:THe DuchesS aNd FrieNdS?

Danny led us down a street and up a road until we reached a wooded area. The trees were gnarled with a black, moist fungus that grew up each trunk and along the limbs and twigs. Some trees had furry leaves, and others had only branches but were so close together, and the trees were so tall that they blocked out most of the grey, hazy sunlight. A cobblestone path wound from the road and into the forest of ugly trees, and it was this path that we took.

Now, I knew where scary fairy tales about witches eating children, pigs building houses, and wolves chasing little girls and chowing down on grandmas came from.

Instead of squirrels, rats and mice darted about the detritus of the ground, climbing up and away onto the tree limbs to watch us, twittering and hissing as we walked along. I waved my procured baseball bat at several, making some of them dart away.

Limmerfer took a stance, puffed out his fur, and hissed angrily. When a rat came too close, he batted it with his claws, sending the rodent flying away with its stomach pierced. Limmerfer looked around as if daring another to come near.

"Way to go, Lim," I said. I petted him on his head.

Danny urged us to be quiet as we approached, "Ahead is the house. Alice, Dana, Pax, and I will go inside.

Annie, you look around the foyer, and stay out of sight. The rest of you stay alert, and yell for us if you see a great army of demons coming or something that looks like an arrest party. We should be able to handle everything inside."

"I have it," Virgil said.

Danny opened the big iron door, and we followed him inside the house. The foyer had been decorated with several open coffins, stone statues of Caligula, Nero, and Julius Caesar, an iron maiden, and various devices hanging from the walls. Skulls on pedestals filled the rest of the room.

"She's a bit of a hoarder," Danny explained.

"No kidding…weird stuff, too," I agreed.

I almost yelled as a figure appeared in the doorway. When I realized it was a servant dressed in a fancy suit with tails on the jacket and a silk tie, I nearly relaxed but then made an '*eeeep*' sound as I saw him in the candlelight.

He had the face of a fish, a catfish, with gills on his neck. There was no nose only a protrusion of his jowls into a flat snout, wide, thin lips surrounded by long, catfish whiskers, and he had no chin. His skin was mottled brown, shaped into scales. There was no forehead or hair, but atop his head was a silly wig powdered and arranged in white curls like those worn long ago by Englishmen. In back, the fake hair was tied into a little ponytail with a silk ribbon in mauve that matched his tie and waistcoat.

His eyes were dull, projecting orbs that tiredly roved over us. He yawned with his great fish mouth, "You must be here to see the Duchess?"

"Of course," Danny said. We nodded.

"From the Queen to the Duchess, I have an invitation to play croquet." Danny held up an envelope to show us. A royal seal was stuck to the back.

"Well, doesn't that sound fun?" I asked.

"Not if you knew them both," Danny whispered.

We followed the servant, ignoring the brackish scent that wafted behind him, despite the powder we had used. Without the powder, the scent would have almost knocked us out.

Another servant appeared, also dressed in a fancy suit, but his hair ribbon and tie were of soft yellow silk. His curls were powdered white, too, but that's where the resemblance ended. His head was huge, topped with that white hair, and covered by crumbly looking warts all over his dark green skin. His mouth was a wide maw without lips and ran from side to side. His eyes were large, protruded slightly, and blinked lazily in his frog face.

With no warning, his thin, long tongue popped out and zapped the side of my face and went back inside his mouth, "Oh, there was a bit of dirt. So sorry."

"You should be. How rude," I snarled at him.

"An invitation from the Queen to the Duchess to play croquet," Fish-Boy said.

Frog-Boy nodded his big head, "From the Queen to the Duchess, an invitation for croquet."

I heard Danny and Pax sigh.

We walked into the dining area where the Duchess held a baby. She glanced up but kept her eyes on the cook.

From where we stood, we could see into the kitchen, as well where Cook prepared a meal in a huge iron pot. Cook tossed in a handful of black pepper that made us all sneeze; she brushed her hands off on her dirty apron.

We all sneezed.

After Fish-Boy handed over the invitation from the Queen, I cleared my throat, "In there on the hearth, that cat…why does he grin that way? I've never seen a cat smile."

"It's my cat, Cheshire. He always grins that way for he's always up to mischief," Duchess said.

I didn't quite trust the cat and wished Limmerfer had come with us to deal with him if he became unruly.

"I told you about cats and hell," Danny said. He threw up an arm just in time to avoid a carving knife that Cook threw across the kitchen and dining room. It landed in the wall behind the Duchess.

We scooted out of the way as Cook threw more utensils, knives, pots, and pans. The Duchess struggled to hold the screaming baby and knock away items that flew past them, "If you don't know about the cats, then you don't know much."

"I'm new here."

"We're all new here," Pax said, "and that's too much pepper." He sneezed again.

A knife almost cut off the baby's nose.

"*Speak roughly to your little boy, And beat him when he sneezes, He only does it to annoy, Because he knows it teases,*" the Duchess sang her poem.

She walked out of the room, spoke in whispers to her Frog-Boy and Fish-Boy, and then seemed to notice the child. We followed her.

She tossed the baby to Dana who barely caught it and told Dana that she could care for it since she was going to play croquet with the Queen. I wondered what we would do with a baby. A child was one thing, but now we had been given a baby in hell.

In another room, Duchess dressed herself in jewels and fancy silk cloth over a dress that was clearly too tight and too sexy for her age and figure.

Danny caught her arm, "You promised me something."

"I did? I don't recall…."

She was a nasty looking woman, and I didn't like her at all.

"Don't try to bullshit me, Duchess, please. If you don't give me what you promised, then I will be happy to whisper into certain ears…let's see…The Board of Artistic Destruction, and you won't get those statues you ordered of Sterkus Berzerkus, Festus Shittus, and Fatt ButtFuckass."

"You wouldn't dare."

"I would."

They traded threats with stern voices. Pax and I covered our mouths to keep from laughing hysterically at the ridiculous names. Those could not possibly be real, I told myself.

"Fine, Take it. But there will be…well…hell to pay," Duchess smirked.

"Trust me, I have paid well and will pay still," Danny said.

Duchess handed over a small velvet bag. As her hand dropped the bag in Danny's hand, we heard a terrible wailing from another room, and Duchess smiled, "Here is your little trinket. This ensures you will not speak of my statues, yes? Your word, please."

"My word," Danny said. He checked the bag and drew out the biggest iolite gemstone I had ever seen. The purple-blue stone was as large as a hen's egg and cut into so many perfect facets one could get dizzy looking into it. Slipping it back into its bag, he put the gem into his pocket, frowned, and looked confused.

"The items you procured for me were simply lovely. I suppose I did owe you that little trifle. But I owe you not a bit more, and walking into my home unbidden was a grievous, most abominable, rude-as-heck act on your part."

"You wouldn't have opened the door and have seen us otherwise, and we couldn't have gotten the gemstone," Danny said.

"Exactly. But alas, you have, and as I said, it was a very offensive action, and I repay in kind. Now, I have plans," she said as she turned and left the room.

Hurrying after her, Dana asked about the baby. What was she to do with it? When would the Duchess be back to care for it? Where should we leave it?

The Duchess waved us away as if she didn't care. The top of her head was bald with only fluffs of frizzy strands above large, ears that stuck out comically. Her eyes were little, and her nose was large and spread out across her face. The lower half of her face was enormous, with a tiny knob of a chin and colorless, tiny, thin lips. Little black whiskers sprouted from her white skin. Wrinkles lined her face, and they, along with rolls of fat, filled her neck. She wiggled in her very low cut, strapless dress that accentuated her heavy body and flabby arms, breasts, and back. She shook her backside at us and giggled.

"She's despicable," I said.

"Does this baby look like her?" Dana showed us the baby wrapped in a blanket.

It had tiny eyes, and I thought its nose resembled a snout; it grunted. As they watched it, it began to look more and more like a piglet and less like a baby. Dana sat it down when its hands and feet looked like trotters.

We went back to the kitchen to tell Cook where we had left the pig (or baby, depending on one's view). Blood and globs of fat were all over the kitchen, so we had to watch where we walked. "What a mess."

Cook glanced at me, "Yes, *she* is."

Danny walked over to a cabinet and reached for something. I saw a glint of metal and realized it was his pocket watch.

"Why was it here?" I asked.

"I noticed it missing while we were with the Duchess and feared the worst, but it was too late by then. I saw the footman pick it up from the floor when we were in the other room; it was left in the hallway."

"How did it get there?"

Dana slapped a hand to her face, "I have taken it away from Annie at least ten times and have given it back to Danny."

"Oh, She pick-pockets?" Pax asked.

"Why was it on the cabinet?"

Danny looked into my eyes with a very sad glance. He turned to the cook and cocked his head, "Supper?"

"Aye."

All at once, I noticed more things about the room. A boot peeked out from beneath a small table. A bag that Annie carried was half hidden by bowls on the counter. The cook raised her cleaver and snapped it down on a delicate hand sitting on the cutting board. In the pot, a human foot bounced around in the boiling water, alongside a whole onion and a skinny carrot.

With a powerful lunge, I kicked the knife away from Cook's hand and followed my kick with a rough push that slammed Cook against the cabinets, "How could you?"

"They brought her in. Meats is meats."

Pax heaved.

The first time I hit her across the throat with the big cleaver, she slid to the ground, grabbing for her neck as slippery blood poured out the wound.

I didn't mind chopping off fingers and then her wrist as I tried to chop off her head. It takes a lot of work to chop through a neck, and Pax came forward, took the cleaver, and began to work, "Off with your head," he said.

Dana and Danny used towels to carry the noxious pot out the back door, into the garden, and away from the house.

Poor Annie. I let tears roll down my cheeks as I went to find Frog-Boy and Fish-Boy. At the threat of my machete, I walked them outside and ordered them to dig a hole. Had I not needed their labor, I would have chopped them to little bits.

Pax finished cutting the head cut off the cook and stabbed her with her own carving forks as a last insult; we wanted to use her own tools to hurt her.

Pax and Danny helped dig, so the work digging a grave went fast, and we buried Annie deeply inside the ground. I made the hideous footmen pick armloads of the Duchess' prized roses and other flowers to cover the grave, leaving stems and bushes barren of posies.

That would teach her.

In glee, I tossed every chemical I found, as well as salt on the flower bushes that were left so they'd never grow beautiful flowers again. We left the cook in the kitchen, along with the blood and mess. Pax and Danny, using the shovels, beat the footmen to red, slimy paste that oozed into the spongy grass.

I took Annie's bag but nothing else.

Danny did take a few things from the kitchen: some bread, butter, and fruit so we could eat, as well as a pitcher of goat's milk, and some glasses.

Outside, we told Coral, Virgil, Cassie, Dinah, and Cory the bad news, and we were solemn as we went down the walkway, along the road, and to a small park, which had benches and a table where we could sit and eat.

You would think we wouldn't be able to eat after that, and it was true that it sickened us, but we also had used a lot of energy and were hungry. I couldn't have eaten boiled meat, of that I am sure.

After we filled our stomachs, we told them everything, trying to say it in less gory ways so no one would get ill. Dinah wept against Cassie. Taking each of our hands in one of hers, Cassie gave us a heartfelt look and said, "I am so very sorry for the loss of your friend. She was a lovely girl, brave, and kind."

Chapter Nineteen: Confession Is Good For the Soul

"Danny, what will happen to her soul?" Cory asked. We had all been wondering that same question.

"It will be as if she were never born, and her soul will be reborn in another body so she has a new chance. I know it's horrible to lose a friend, but she isn't lost here. She has not had a chance yet to clean her slate, and so she will have a new one."

"Good," I said, but I still wept.

Danny told us, "Confession is good for the soul, and she confessed to me weeks ago that she liked stealing my watch. It became a game for us."

Dana nodded, "I want to tell all of you something."

I nodded.

"Alice...everyone, I had that pelvic infection from a bad abortion. The man the pregnancy was with gave me a drug in my drink one night and took me to a doctor who practiced medicine in the basement of his home; he was a very bad doctor, and his home wasn't very clean, I suppose. That was why I became so sick and almost died."

I hugged her, "Dana, surely that wouldn't get you bad marks on your tally board. Danny, how is that fair? She was drugged. She didn't agree to it."

Danny nodded, "It's true she didn't agree, and she doesn't have marks for *that.*"

"I have bad marks because the man was my professor, and he was married, and I knew it. I made a terrible choice in that matter. I regret it for so many reasons...." Dana confessed.

"Will this clean her slate, Danny?"

"If we succeed, yes. If not, she must try something else if she has a chance. I hope she cleans it, really," Danny said.

I squeezed Dana's hand.

Coral spoke, "I used drugs when I was playing football. I didn't plan to use them, but steroids were all around, and then…worse: when I was high, I hit my wife until she ran away to keep me from hurting her. I also was in a few driving accidents that hurt people badly and were covered up by people who handle those kinds of things. I regretted it when I got sober and ruined my knee and was a wash-up."

"Oh, Coral." Cassie patted his hand.

"That's why I don't drink at all, and I make sure homeless are fed. But I need to clear my slate."

"Annie was a thief, a kleptomaniac," I said.

"I coveted. I was a mean, petty, jealous man who only wanted to get ahead. I had a friend who was the same way, and one day, his house burned to the ground. I stood and watched it blaze from the sidewalk. He was upset and furious about what he had lost: his BMW, his expensive suits, his beautiful furniture, and I was jolted like lightning had hit me," Pax told us.

"Why?" Coral asked.

"Because his wife and son were in the house. I was there to comfort him but wasn't going to once he said that. It made me sick, but I realized that I had acted the same way, as if *stuff* mattered so much. I sold everything I had and headed out across the United States, taking only what I could carry and taking my dog, Katie. I gave everything away."

"Wow, I never knew, Paxton," I said softly, amazed that my friends had such traumatic events in their pasts, "Cory?"

"Hmmm?"

"What about you? What all are you making up for?"

"Why ask me? I'm along for the fun. I don't have terrible secrets," he said.

I wondered what he didn't want to tell us. I also wondered why he didn't share since everyone else had talked.

Cassie hugged me and promised I could fulfill this mission and would do a great job. Her faith in me helped.

"We have a place to sleep tonight, but it's a bit of a bother. A man said we could stay there, and we can, but a few squatters always like to take over and stay there as well. Once we arrive, we will see if we can charm them and get them to leave or share."

"We could just chop them to bits," I said, waving my machete.

"We could, but remember they'd regenerate and rat us out, I fear. We'll do better to get along with them if we possibly can. Let's hurry. We're in dinosaur territory, and they come out at night. I prefer to avoid them," Danny said, walking faster.

Chapter Twenty: Insane Institution:

I saw a sign as we went into the large building, Insane Institution. I asked Danny why we were going to this place, and he said this was where he had been speaking of and this would provide a place to sleep for the night.

"And why are the squatters here?"

Virgil laughed, "They've never left, really."

They introduced us to Ed March-Hare and Stan Hatter, both humans, as far as I could tell, but at this point, I wasn't sure about much and still felt Annie's loss deeply. I was cranky as we sat down at a table, and Danny motioned for the pair to pour us some hot tea.

"Drink the wine instead," Ed March-Hare told us.

"Is there wine?" Danny asked.

"No."

"Then why did you offer it?"

March-Hare glared, "I didn't. I simply suggested it. You sat down uninvited, and I offered wine that isn't."

"No matter," Danny went on, "we're staying here the night. I hope we don't bother you too much."

"Oh no, not here. We're here," Stan Hatter frowned hatefully.

"You can't stay. It would be like saying *you'll stay if you're happy* is the same as saying *that you are happy if you stay*. You won't be happy either way. And you can't stay," March-Hare said, confusing everyone.

"The dinosaurs are roaming, so we have no choice," Danny told them.

"You have no dinosaurs either as your choices are roaming."

Coral shrugged, "True."

Stan Hatter didn't argue, "Do you realize you have a big worm with you?"

"The worm in the apple catches the bird," March-Hare announced.

"He must be early though," Stan added.

"Yes, early apples are best. But back to the worm…."

"No shit. You think we need to go back to that subject?" Cory muttered, "but she's our friend."

"You shit, and there is no thinking," March-Hare said.

Stan Hatter agreed, "No thinking at all. No wonder he missed the apple."

"Why are the insane in hell?" I asked Virgil and Danny, tired of their games and word play. I snatched the tea pot away and poured it in the cups while Dana got more water and set a pot to boil so she could make more. We both stomped around a lot.

"They are insane, but they are also naughty. Stan was downright deadly when he burned down a school and killed five kids and injured a dozen. They said he was insane, but he was pretending. He was evil. Being down here so long and the smells I told you about have caused his insanity," Danny said.

"I don't know why I'm here, but that reason is as good as any," Stan Hatter said, "I'll take it, so mark it down."

Danny went on, "Ed March-Hare worked alongside Jack-the-Ripper in England long ago. Sometimes, he whispers the name of the killer. He's not good with secrets. They say he fell mad after seeing the first demon, but I don't know if that is so. Is it? Ed?"

Ed only shrugged, "Did I see a demon? Maybe so."

Danny grinned slyly, "Looky, what I have." He held up small, amber, plastic bottles for the men to see. Both sat up straight and looked contrite.

"In the morning if you do as I say, I will give you each a bottle, and we'll be on our way. If you give us trouble, we'll toss you to the dinosaurs."

And as if to make my point, outside one of the dinosaurs let loose with a terrible roar.

After both men nodded, Danny said, "Find a good pork roast, and make sure it is really pig and not human. I can tell. Find us good vegetables, bread, and fruit, maybe some butter, real chicken's eggs, and make it quick. Cook dinner for us, and tell us when it's ready."

"For the pills? That's all?" Stan Hatter rose.

"Some more tea, and then we'll want a nice warm fire and pallets of clean linens and pajamas. While we sleep, I want our clothing and boots cleaned properly."

Ed March-Hare got to his feet, "We'll be back in a jiffy. I think we've an old tub back there if you don't mind lukewarm water from the taps and hand made soap."

We guarded the building when the men ran off to do as Danny commanded.

When it was my turn, I began filling the tub, undressed quickly, and wrapped myself in a short towel as I waited for someone to bring me the pail of hot water to add to the tub.

To my embarrassment, Virgil brought the pail of near-boiling water with steam rising around the handle. I froze in place and was aware of his eyes traveling from my feet to my face. Taking time to savor each detail. My face flamed, but I also felt a funny tickle and buzz in my nether regions, which embarrassed me further.

"Oh, I brought your water," he said as looked flustered too, something he never looked.

"I was just getting ready for my bath."

He poured the water into the tub, avoiding looking at me. Was I ugly? Probably so. He had looked me over, and maybe I was still fat or proportioned oddly, or maybe I was okay until he got to my head. My hair was too dark, or my face was plain.

I felt hurt. I wasn't angry with him, but at myself for being unattractive. "You can leave now so you don't have to look at my ugliness. Seriously," I snapped. I was ashamed I had even considered he might like me.

"Huh?"

"Just leave."

I took my time in submerging myself. The soap smelled of fat and a dark, old spice, but I tried not to think about it as I bathed myself clean.

It wasn't the sort of bath to spend extra time enjoying, so once clean, I dried myself and yanked on soft clothing the men had brought: inmates' pants, shirt, and socks. Plain clothing. Asexual. It fit me.

After I carefully tipped over the tub and emptying the water, I called for Pax, who, after having drawn a straw, was next in line. He noticed I was down and asked what was wrong, but I waved it off, saying I was just tired and ugly.

"Ugly? What?"

"Nothing."

"How do you feel, Dinah?"

"Better," she said and smiled. *"Twinkle, twinkle, little lass; We will eat you mighty fast; Down our throats you will fly; You'll be better once you die,"* she sang.

"That's terrible, Honey. Where did you hear it?" Cassie asked.

"The man who kept us on chains sang it a lot."

I reached over and wiped away a tear that rolled down Dinah's cheek, "That won't happen. We're far from him now."

I wanted to go back and cut the man's arms off again. That he would reincarnate, albeit without arms because they were quickly stolen and taken to trade or to eat, didn't make me feel a bit better. He had the propensity to keep doing evil.

"Her parents were so poor the father sold himself to the Flensing Stations and then her mother did the same. They were both suicides in the old world, way back evidently because Dinah describes their clothing as very odd, maybe Roman like."

We talked to Dinah and Cassie, straightened pallets with the blankets and linens that only smelled a little musty to us, and waited for our dinner.

Before long, the two men brought us plates of food; the food looked wonderful; both of them belched often, so no doubt they had already eaten. The roast was not good like Coral's roasts, but it was passable as was the bread, purplish peas, red squash, and pale blue potatoes. The odd colors confused us a lot, but everything tasted just fine.

"They get bored here, and so they grow food of odd colors. It's perfectly fine," Virgil reassured us. I ignored him.

I thought that made sense. All had been here for a very long time, at least some had, and they didn't have much change from day-to-day and knew they would have the same forever; that alone made my head throb with confusion. I could understand that people here grew bored and wanted anything to be different and interesting.

That idea made me think of myself since I had always craved sameness and the mundane, never showing curiosity or interest in anything. No wonder poor Dana hadn't told me about her terrible ordeal.

Instead of appreciating and dealing with changes and interesting events, both positive and negative, I had tried to insulate myself and hide from everything in life. What a sinful thing I had done.

In the morning and well rested, we rose to finish the tea, bread, butter, and fruit, along with omelets that Coral made with left over vegetables. Our clothing had been cleaned, and our boots were polished; we dressed again, feeling clean and satiated.

Outside, Limmerfer hissed at noxious pile.

"Velociraptors," Danny told us, "they must have our scent which means we must be very careful at night now, or they will attack any place we hide."

"What were those pills?" I asked.

"Anti-psychotics. They think things will be better for them when they take the medication and can think clearly, but it will actually be much worse as they come to terms with where they are. I had no particular love for them. We needed something. They wanted something. I don't care what it is they want."

"Why is the sanatorium closed? Did everyone but those few get better or...?" Dana asked as she skirted a big pile around what looked like animal droppings.

Danny chuckled, "Think backwards. An Institute for Insanity doesn't *help* people, silly goose; it provides medication, counseling, shock therapy, torture, and behavioral therapy to *incite* insanity. They have about a ninety-nine point ninety-nine percent success rate in causing acute depression, sociopathy, schizophrenia, and manias."

"Why did you dress like a rock and roll singer when you came to the diner the first night, Danny?"

"It annoyed you. It was a start and better than no reaction at all."

I snickered, "I've thought about that. I am going to begin taking an interest in life from now on. It's a waste to be so apathetic."

"Good to know that." Danny chewed his lip. "Now, you may have sympathy for some we'll see today, but hold yourself back.

Here, this is business as usual, and you can't really save anyone even as bad things happen, and they can't die and find release."

"So I should watch torture?"

"You may save them this second, but they will be tortured a billion-zillion times more after you walk away. One time gives them false hope if anything, Alice."

Chapter Twenty-One: King Henry VIII: King of Hearts

I mulled that over as we walked. Sometimes, the path was nothing but a packed, dirt road; sometimes it was littered with hay; other times it was a burned, wide spot that we walked across, listening to the dead grass crinkle. It sounded as if we were walking on shards of ice. Bad roads were a hell-thing, too, it seemed.

Danny and Virgil showed us a building that finally wasn't dull grey concrete but was of layered, hand-sized scales of obsidian, a volcanic glass that the Aztecs once used a long time ago for tips on spears and for knives. The glass could be cut so thin and fine that it cut like a razor. Thin pieces were overlapped and layered on the building so anyone, bumping it or leaning against it, would be shredded.

Inside, the floor was the same obsidian, but it was cut into beautiful squares that were separated with blocks of lapis and thin lines of mother-of-pearl. The walls, lit brightly with candles, were plastered and painted light blue. On some walls, azure silk curtains rustled in the breeze and on others, enormous paintings hung and depicted sea scenes. The room felt tranquil.

It was the perfect foil for the gigantically obese man dressed in red, gold, and white. Every move he made: a raise of his hand or a half turn, caught our attention.

A contingency of women and men knelt at his feet, all dressed in shades of blue so they melted into the décor. One woman was rather dour-faced, dark and tiny; another was pale with witchy, long black hair and flashing black eyes; a third had soft brown hair and a sweet face.

"Who are they?"

"King Henry and his wives. Many times a week, a big ceremony is held, and he sends them to be punished all together, or alone, and sometimes along with various men who have been disloyal. The dark one who is smirking? That is Anne Bolen. They cut off her head, and then they replace it again until the next time. Once, they put Anne's head on backwards; that was funny," Danny said.

"Not to her," Coral growled.

"Maybe not, but it really was funny to see that."

"Off with her head," Henry shouted, his crown sliding sideways. He pointed to random women as he yelled that many times.

"Is the Duchess here? I have some payback for her," Dana whispered.

Henry spun, "The Duchess? Are you her friend?"

Dana held her head high, "I am certainly not. She's a vile murderess, as well as a stinking, sneaky bitch, and a sick, twisted sadist."

"Indeed? Well, we won't gloat about her *positive* points. Off with the Duchess' head, too." Henry rambled about the room. And for no apparent reason, Henry spewed, "And the cats. I want their heads removed. And the gardeners, too."

"It seems they'll all be headless soon," I remarked.

"And? Do you approve?"

"I don't disapprove, but you won't remove the head from our cat as he is our friend."

"Are you friends with our gardeners?"

"No, your Royal Highness," I said.

"Then, why did you bring it up?" asked Henry. Henry again showed his dementia.

"Me? I…I have not one concern over the gardeners. I see some weeds, so evidently they're not doing their jobs if there are weeds in the lawn."

The king sniffed, "Pull those weeds, and then go get beheaded. We should do things in order, I think. Don't get busy and forget the beheading part…."

I covered a laugh.

"What do you want here? I'm very busy," King Henry asked.

I felt my muscles tense. Was it almost time to fight?

Danny reached into his coat and removed a small box made of tin and set with a glass top, like an odd paperweight. It was as large as his hand, and he showed the king what he had, "We want a mere nobody from your prison, a girl named Ellie. For her, I will give you this."

Henry VIII ran a finger over the box, sniffed at it, and licked his lips lasciviously, "A virgin's heart. How lovely…what a novelty."

"I know you like hearts and this one…lovely, yes? So pure…so perfect," Danny prodded.

"A mere nobody. Why are you interested enough in her to offer me such a priceless trade?" the king asked.

Danny shrugged, "Do we have a deal? The girl, Ellie, is new here and a little lost and silly. But her innocence," he breathed softly, making his voice almost obscene, "it is interesting to me."

"Tom, contact the prison, and see if this girl is still alive. Return, and tell me if she is there." The king waved us away and told us that we could wait there while they played games on the lawn.

Following them, we found the entire royal entourage sitting about playing a game. A table of food was available, but we asked about each dish before sampling, afraid we might be fed something or someone, right?

In a few minutes, the king came over to us and said that when the servant confirmed that the girl was in the prison, which was very far away in the very heart of hell, we would have a deal.

He would give us a letter to release her. He looked over his subjects, and then, he turned to us, "Quite a bore, if you ask me, but then you didn't. It's a trade."

Danny handed him the box, and we tried to make our leave, hesitating as we left because the trumpets blared and the crowd gathered. The Queen shrilled at us, "You can't leave, now. The show is on. You must stay now."

Dutifully, we sat down among the others as the servants wheeled out a strange device. It was more like a giant stage made of wood and rolled out with massive wheels; in the center of the stage sat a guillotine, its wickedly sharp blade glittering dangerously.

Two men wheeled out a cart and threw hay up onto the stage; it would soak up the blood.

The king looked at our confusion and told us, "Ann gave birth to a daughter if you can believe that, and then, she couldn't give birth to a normal, live baby, much less a prince. Her two spawns were half-formed, dead, and hideous when they should have been male heirs."

"Isn't the male responsible for a child's gender," I whispered to Dana.

She nodded.

Henry went on, "She used witchcraft to seduce me. You can look into her eyes and see the evil. And now, she's to be beheaded for high treason, adultery with no less then fifteen men, and incest with her brother."

"All praise be, her *remarkable* traits," a man in a black robe intoned.

"Yes, those things are quite respected here but," he said as laughed, "off with her head!"

"Why is she in hell?" Pax asked.

The man in black looked bored, "She made the good king a heretic. Simple. She forced him to break with the church in order to procure a divorce from Catherine to marry her."

I thought back to my history lessons. It seemed to me that he had chased Anne and decided to divorce Catherine on his own. He was the one who had made the choice.

"Off with her head…cut it off…let the heads roll."

Anne walked up the scaffolding as she had countless times before, trying to keep her head up. Her servants took her necklaces, and she gave a speech, declaring the king to be a kind, gentle man, despite the fact that he had sent her to the guillotine.

She knelt, her red petticoat shining and swishing loudly, and in one swoop, her head was severed and went rolling across the stage, leaking blood. Not a sound escaped her lips during the beheading. Her maids wailed.

King Henry stood, applauded, and gathered the royal party and walked back to the mansion, leaving us behind with the head, a few guards, and one another.

I didn't want to see them take the head and reattach it so she could do this again.

The servant came back with news, whispered it to the king, and he nodded. After calling for ink and paper, he scrawled orders on the paper, waved it to dry the ink, folded it, and handed it to Danny, "The trade is done."

We made our way back to the road, and I thought about Henry, the King of Hearts. I wondered how he could be called King of Hearts since he was heartless.

Chapter Twenty-Two: Second Circle of Hell

We walked along the road, some of our boots making little tapping sounds. For a few minutes, a yellowy, sulfuric rain fell, and a few demon children cavorted, dancing in the stinking liquid.

In a few minutes, the children's reptilian, dark bodies were covered with a fine sheen of yellow. They opened their mouths and let the drops fill their mouths.

Lightning exploded in the distance, making the smoggy brown clouds light up. If the storm came closer, we'd have to take cover.It never did, so we walked along the road when the nasty rain stopped and ducked under trees or into a stall.

"This is the Second Circle of Hell," Virgil told us, "it's for lovers who have sinned."

He pointed out an Egyptian area in the distance where laborers built a pyramid. They sweated and struggled to pull and push stones into place, but it was never finished, as their queen demanded it to be built taller, larger, and more magnificent. The monument was already the largest pyramid that the travelers had ever seen, and Virgil said it was four times as large as any in their world.

"Who was the queen?" Coral asked.

"Cleopatra. She had many lovers, deceived all of them, and seduced them with her beauty and sorcery, so she lives all alone and when a would-be lover tries to visit her, they both break out in boils," Virgil told us.

"Interesting," Dana said.

Chapter Twenty-Three: Sobek's Crocs

Danny interrupted, "Keep alert. We will be skirting the river, and Sobek's crocodiles bask there. They are faster than you'd think and have a bite force of five thousand pounds. They can chase down many animals and people and devour them…vicious things at best. Crocodiles are very dangerous."

"That's a lot of bite force, isn't it?" Cassie asked.

"People fear pit bulls, and they have a bite force of about five hundred pounds, and a great white shark has a force of about five *hundred* pounds."

Coral frowned at Danny, "They bite harder than a shark? Damn."

Danny nodded, "But some of the dinos can bite five times harder than a croc. You see why I avoid the bastards?"

Coral made a motion with his hands. "Walk softly. I see them."

Along the sandy, muddy beach and amid a few skinny, pitiful-looking trees, lay scores of vicious-looking crocodiles, their roughly scaled bodies showing as a texture in the mud. As we passed, several moved lazily, raising their long snouts to sniff at us. Big teeth showed, and they shook their heads back and forth.

One, and he was every bit seven feet long, snapped at a smaller crocodile, making it waddle out of the mud in the strange way they walked, as if their hips were set wrong. The smaller reptile winked an eye at us, his vertical pupil contracting. He watched us.

"They've noticed us," Pax whispered.

"Keep going," Danny urged us, "we really don't want to have to fight them."

We almost heard a horrible sound. I say *almost* because it wasn't so much a sound as it was a vibration in the air, a rumbling and displacement that was too deep for us to catch with our ears, but we felt it. "What was that?"

Virgil grabbed my elbow and hurried me along.

"They push air out of their voice boxes, causing their muscles to vibrate violently. All the crocs in the water heard it very clearly as sound and felt the vibration; it said food was walking around and would be easy to eat. The sound was too low for us to hear but see Lim? He's scared."

The cat's fur stood on end as he ran beside us.

"The croc definitely called to the rest. He announced dinner."

Virgil stopped as a dozen of the creatures came at us, telling us we couldn't outrun them. We formed a line in front of Cassie and Dinah.

"Sobek, if you are here, we are travelers and wish no trouble. We mean no harm and wish to pass by," Danny called in case the Egyptian god was listening.

"Danny, we didn't train for crocodile fights, did we?" I asked sarcastically.

"Hold steady. As one unit, back away to the direction we were going," Danny ordered. We did as he said, watching the creatures cautiously, although if they attacked, I would have no idea what to do.

The croc stared us down, and a few others raised their ugly heads to look at us from the mud. Reptile droppings have a particularly sharp musky, wild scent that one can sometimes get a whiff of in a zoo, and again, I was glad my sense of smell was deadened because what I could smell was rank. With the droppings, various decayed victims, bacteria, and rotting vegetation, the mud was a hot bed of nastiness, and yet Danny whispered that it was used by spas that demons loved. I couldn't imagine much worse.

Whether Sobek took pity on us or we were lucky, the crocodiles lost interest and sauntered jerkily back to their mud hole as we backed away.

In a few minutes, the man-eaters were far behind us, and we were able to breathe sighs of relief. Danny said that if they had attacked, we would have been in trouble. The only ones of us surviving would have been those who ran while the rest were consumed. Depressing.

Chapter Twenty-Four: Carnage: Don't Look Back

Next, we came to a village, a crumbling Greek-looking settlement. Virgil said we had come at a good time because Helen of Troy and Sparta was sleeping or otherwise engaged. Usually, she would be throwing mirrors and screaming like a banshee while she tried to decide between her Spartan husband, Menelaus; her true love, Theseus: her later love, Paris; her lover, Hector; or her rapist, Deiphobus.

Coral replied, "I don't understand her actions."

Virgil explained, "In the village streets, the men often fought over Helen, the most beautiful woman on earth. He said she was also a part-time vampire who hunted a few nights out of each month. Many men lustily looked forward to being chosen and then to being bitten; she was very attractive and sexy, but when she looked in the mirror, she saw a monster."

"You saw the Amazon queen earlier, and no doubt she comes here to wreak vengeance on Achilles. It's like what you, back home, call a drama or a soap opera. It would make your head ache, trying to figure out who was involved with whom," Danny told us.

"There sure a lot of kings and queens here in hell," I said.

"Yes, there are; makes you wonder a little."

We saw a wall that stretched a mile in the distance. Men and a few women hung from ropes around their wrists and had to reach up to stand on their tiptoes. Their eyes were brutally scraped from the sockets, and blood ran down their faces. Horrible creatures ran about, catching the eyes with their jaws and swallowing them whole or crunching into them.

The creatures looked like women with stringy, matted hair, but had flat, sagging breasts, were forced to walk on their hands, and raise their heads up, stretching their necks as their hind quarters were those of dogs or hyenas. It was a struggle just to make sense of their forms so matted was their fur and flea-covered bodies.

"The men and women on the wall were pornographers; their eyes grow back several times a day. They filmed for others to see depravity, child abuse, terrible things, and so they were doomed to lose their own eyes for eternity."

"And the dog women?" I asked Virgil.

"Porn stars, they lay down with dogs, so to speak, like wild animals, and they wake with fleas. If they were so depraved in their work, so will they be here," Virgil said, "this is the circle of lust and seduction. Mind your desires here."

Prostitutes were everywhere around us.

"Hey, you wanna good time," one asked.

"Nope. Just passing through," Coral replied.

"You know, denying your desires is an offense here. Refusing debauchery is against the law," a hooker in a skintight purple outfit declared.

"Then, we'll be secretive about it, okay?" Pax said.

They were gathering like birds in all colors: amethyst skintight latex, bright blue satin, crimson short shorts and halter, canary yellow tight pants and tube top, emerald slip dress with shining sequins, orange flowing gown like fire. All were beautiful women, and even the demoness hookers were alluring with wide, generous hips, lush breasts, and sultry glances.

Miss Orange waved a finger, "No. We are here to ensure the letter of the law is followed. Pick your treat, and let's get busy."

"Back off," Cory warned.

I saw that he, like the other men, was a little glassy-eyed. The women were very attractive and sexy in smoky ways. I glared. "Last warning, and then we're going to push through," I said.

"Baby, come push me," Miss Emerald purred, "Ummm...push me until I scream with happiness; I like take-control types."

I had enough. With little concern, I snapped a kick that landed my foot right under Miss Orange's chin, making her teeth clack together.

Before I was even out of my stance, I swung my pipe into Purple's head, enjoying how her noggin popped backwards.

Dana was facing off the chick in blue, punching and kicking.

Coral was wrestling two women dressed in black, trying to get in position to crack their necks while Pax and Yellow Girl ducked and kicked violently.

Before I could think, I saw half dozen prostitutes run at us from a house and then another half dozen fly out from behind a building. They carried swords or long knives. After I slammed a kick into a hooker's arm and flipped her over, I grabbed her lost sword and shoved it into her heart, ending that battle.

All around me, my friends had done the same, taking weapons and using them on the offenders, stabbing, cutting, and chopping.

When we finally stopped the fight, a few heads, many arms, and a few legs littered the street as blood ran in thick pools to the canals. Danny had a nasty wound on his arm he said he had gotten when one swiped a sword at him, and Pax said his ankle felt achy from a wrong landing as he back kicked a demoness.

Two men shyly approached us. "Hello."

"Hi," I said, "you with them?"

"Oh, no. But now that you're done, will you be needing them or can…ummm…we have them?" the stranger asked.

"You want them?" I asked, disgusted again. They looked at the torn bodies and smiled at them lasciviously, licking their lips. I didn't know if it were for food or sex and didn't want to know. "Have at 'em."

We walked down the street, not looking back at the carnage, and I have no idea what happened to the two men or the scraps of hookers we left behind.

To my left, another man had his eyes dug out with a dull spoon, and a dog-woman gobbled up the prized orbs greedily.

We passed the Interactive Museum of Rapists where Danny said sightseers could abuse rapists. I thought that was more than fair turn-about for those people.

We saw a building that I didn't understand at all. It was called Pedo-Poop Bricks. Danny said that pedophiles were put into large vats and chained; a tube was inserted into their mouths. They were fed continuously and were kept in the huge vats of excrement at all times. As they digested the food, they added to the supply of feces.

Workers used the feces to mix with mud and construct bricks that were in turn used in buildings. I thought that rather fitting as well.

The final place we saw was a building of glass that we could see inside of. Down the center was another section of glass, and half of the people were on one side, and half were on the other. They stood barefoot on an uncomfortable-looking grate floors.

This was the Untouchable Lovers headquarters, a sort of torturing dating service where men and women came to see their lovers, separated from them by a pane of glass for all time. They could see their true love but never hold or kiss. "Tears fall down the grates and are collected. It is bottled and sold at very high prices," Danny said.

Virgil nodded, "It is said Cleopatra buys cases of the bottles of tears. She rubs the tears on her breasts and hopes that she can grow a heart; her heart is a little lump of coal."

I was glad to leave that strange area.

CHapteR TWeNty-FiVe: CiRCLe oF OveR InduLgeNCe

The next circle, we were told, was the Circle of Over Indulgence. The men said we would have a safe house to stay because no one cared what his neighbor did; everyone cared only for himself here.

I lost track of how many morbid obese men and women waddled down the street, barely able to walk.

In one stall, an alcoholic, with skin falling off his red nose, and eyes, red as his nose and bleeding, had alcohol to sell to alcoholics. Hypodermic needles with various drugs were sold in vending machines.

A greasy man hailed us, "I know your pleasure; I know your weakness," he said.

"Yeah?" Pax muttered.

The greasy man pointed to Dana, "She eats and vomits. I have food, baby doll; wanna go a round of bulimic delight? And you used to hoard, but now you want freedom and crave less and less. Give me everything you carry, and enjoy the fun," he said to Pax.

To Coral, he giggled, "You'd still kill for a drop of...let's see...vodka is your favorite. And you, you crave blood; oh how you love to see the fight and hear the crack of bones," he told Danny.

"And me?" I countered.

"You crave peace, and I suggest buying from me a wee bag of cush.

The cowboy...yes, you...you crave a woman's touch. Can I substitute a delightful, comely demoness that knows thirty-four special ways to thrill a man to take your mind off your desire?

And the last of you....” he laughed at Cory, “You crave much. A hypo of morph, a baggie of cush, a snort of the white lady, a trip that will show you Lucy in the Sky with Diamonds; yes, I know what you crave.”

“I'll pass,” I snarled.

“No, thanks,” Coral growled.

“Screw off,” Danny said.

Virgil blushed, and Dana's face went purple with anger and humiliation.

It was embarrassing to have the man point out secrets and weaknesses in front of everyone.

We picked up our pace, turned down a few roads, and came to a huge house, which looked like a mansion to me.A fat man answered and ushered us in, looking to see if we had been followed.

Danny pulled a small packet from his pocket and said, “Here is your payment.”

The fat man unwrapped the package, saw several packs of gum, and shoved several of sticks at one time.

Smiling broadly, he said, “The kitchen is that way. Pick your rooms, and make yourself at home. I won't be around now that I have this from the living world.” He stroked the packs of gum as if they were treasures, and it was funny.

Gum!

But then, maybe he had missed gum above all.

We found food in the kitchen: a dinosaur roast, which tasted like chicken, but was more gamy and smothered with garlic and herbs. I liked it. We had vegetables and fruit and ended the meal with fruit pies.

Later, we took baths in real tubs with hot water, and I found a bottle of bubbles that smelled like honeysuckle. It was relaxing to submerge myself, wash my hair with the bubbles, and finally feel clean. The fat man had all of this, but he suffered for want the gum.

A skinny servant, covered with tattoos and piercings took our clothing to wash. He had no skin left uncolored or un-pierced that I could see. The females got shapeless, thin silk nightdresses, and the men had pajamas. Even Cassie covered herself in a huge, tent-like sheath of silk and trembled happily at how soft it was.

As they gathered in the hallway, Danny gave them the itinerary for the next day.

Chapter Twenty-Six: Land of the Beggars

"Tomorrow, we go through the Land of the Beggars. False priests and false preachers reside there. In their lives, they stole from their believers by begging for contributions that the fakers used to get rich. They claimed that sending the money would heal the sick and banish the evil of the world, but in reality, their mansions were bigger, their cars shinier, and their jewelry heavier.Now, they beg for coins for food.

One of the false preachers said, " I need money, or I will be called to Heaven."

"You wish." Virgil rolled his eyes.

Kick them away if they become tiresome," Danny said.

Virgil interrupted, "Then, we will catch a boat to go across the River Styx. The fallen angels guard the river. If we are lucky, they'll ignore us, but it may be that they ask us difficult questions. If they do, be clever and sharp, and hope we know the answers."

Chapter Twenty-Seven: Questions and Some Answers

On the second floor, I stood out on the terrace, looking out on hell. I felt terribly homesick, missed my parents, and missed normalcy. I didn't belong here, but then, I suppose all who came to live here felt the same, only they were doomed to be here forever. *How depressing was that?* I think it was getting to me.

I stared out at the land, wondering how people could live here and more of them not go mad, how people could be so evil, and why people didn't at least try to be good down here, and hope something worked.

I mean, whether or not they ever got out, at least they could try to have a less horrible life and not revel in depravity and live with such nastiness. There had to be some in hell who might not be great but still have a few morals and a desire for something less tormenting.

"Are you okay?"

"I guess so. It's sad. It's very sad to see such hopelessness here. I'm not saying they don't deserve it, but I hate seeing the torture," I told Virgil.

He rubbed my back, "You don't belong here. Most people would have crumbled by now from seeing this world. We needed someone as strong as you."

"I'm not so strong," I said.

"You are."

"What world are you and Danny from?" I asked, turning to him.

"Don't ask me that," he said as his eyes looked sad.

"Do you like me?"

He groaned, "Why would you ask that either?"

"I don't know. I feel alone here at times. And I was wondering about it. I do have questions at times, and how will I know if I don't ask?"

Virgil took a deep breath, "I like you more than I have the right to. I would gladly die for you.

When we talked about the assignment, we studied you and discussed you. I got to know you before we ever met. Going from here to there on assignment isn't easy. It's painful, like every muscle and bone is ground to dust.

The pain was so incredible that when we made the transition, I lay on the ground, wishing to die just so the pain would stop. And every day, the pain was almost as bad. And it burned...always burned..."

"I didn't know."

"We hid it. But it was worth it. We are setting things to right." I asked, "Were you unhappy with the assignment? Angry that you got it?"

Virgil smiled sadly, "Angry? Danny was assigned. I volunteered."

"Why? Did you know how painful it would be?"

"Yes, I knew. Alice, you don't get it. I knew you before I met you. I volunteered so I could be with you for this time," his voice went to a whisper, "I loved you before I ever saw you."

I didn't know what to say. I reached out a hand to touch his shirt and faltered. I cared about him, and I wanted him, but it felt as if we were separated by worlds; we were. I stepped closer, hoping that the answer would be there although I didn't know the question.

Before I could think, Virgil was kissing me, and everything else vanished. He was there. I was there. We were in the moment. It wasn't as graceful as one would hope for, but amid giggles and banging into walls, Virgil swept me into his arms and took me to his bed where we made love for hours before sleeping deeply, side by side.

I was able to tell Virgil I loved him, too, and I meant it.

Even in hell, there is love. And isn't that the worst of misery?

CHapter TWeNty-EigHt: StyX aNd StoNes

The River was dark, black as onyx, as it flowed across the land. Three tall beings stood before us, and we had to pass them before we could take the ferry across.

"Hello, Imposers, what do you want? I am Beelzebub." He was human looking, handsome, and had black hair and full features.

The next fallen angel was red haired and fierce looking, "Why do you dare come here? I am Azael."

"I am Wyrmwood. What is it you seek?" The third one looked very gruff.

"We're only travelers."

Azeal glared, "Is that a cat with you? Why did you bring a cat?"

"He is part of our group," Virgil said, scooping Limmerfer into his arms.

Azeal sniffed, "I smell mortal."

"It's of no matter…what is a mere mortal?"

"Indeed, but mortals smell so sweet. I feel my stomach rumbling," Azeal said as he rubbed his heavily muscled belly, "when did I last taste mortal?"

"We're on an important errand, and even Satan himself takes interest in it. Eat the mortals, and you will subject yourself to his wrath, but that is your choice," Danny said.

"Yes, it is our choice," Beelzebub agreed, sniffing the air as well.

I couldn't stop myself from asking a question, "Why are former angels here? How did you end up in hell?"

Wyrmwood grinned, "Look at us. Are we not magnificent? And this is the way we look in hell. When we were angels we were so beautiful that your eyes would have burned away in your heads had you looked at us."

"Oh, it was pride?" I asked.

"No, you ignorant mortal," Beelzebub thundered.

"We were among the most beautiful of all, and what does a handsome man want? A handsome woman," Wyrmwood said.

"A perfect, sensuous, woman with human scents and a warm body…ummm," Beelzebub shivered with delight, making my stomach roll with repugnance.

"I left the confines of…you know," he said as he pointed upwards, "and walked the earth in your world, Mortal. I found many willing women, the daughters of man, and they satiated my cravings. That wasn't allowed, so for my vanity, lust, and pride, I was tossed out to reside here. My brethren here suffered the same indignity for daring to love mortals."

"Oh," I said, "Well, you broke the rules, huh? And I *was* right…it was partially pride."

Wyrmwood nodded, "Can you not see how difficult that was? That rule? Can angels not feel desire? Why should we feel it and be forced to refrain?"

"Because those are the rules," Coral said.

Wyrmwood stared at me, " Now, I find you attractive, mortal. Do you fancy my love?"

I resisted the impulse to puke. They were creepy, and malevolence wafted off them, so I knew lust for mortal women wasn't their only sin. I doubted they were so innocent and thought maybe they had taken advantage of women at the very least.

"She's with me," Virgil said.

Wyrmwood sniffed delicately, and his eyes went dark, "I could take you in battle."

"I don't think you could. If you could, you would have pounced immediately, and yet, you didn't. We'll pass, and you will not touch the mortals with us."

"She is your first mortal love; she was a dream, a taint only; why did you damn yourself, Virgil? For a dream?"

Virgil faced Wyrmwood angrily, "A dream? She is with me."

"For now. She can't remain."

Danny interrupted, "Stop listening to him."

"What does he mean?" I asked.

Azael chuckled, "Secrets, Vine?"

"Vine?" I asked.

Azael nodded, "Your lover is named Vine, and he was once one of the most beautiful angels of all. Some of the others were admonished for impure thoughts of him, but he was absolute perfection.

Vine had no eyes for anyone of the angels, however, but he did his work dutifully until it was noticed that more and more, he was found idle in the gardens, dreaming and lost in his own mind."

Virgil made a huffing sound.

"Vine, or Virgil, as you now know him, dreamed of a mortal woman who was yet to be born, undoubtedly the only reason he didn't act upon his desires and wind up here standing along with the three of us," Azrael chuckled again. "But he no doubt waited for the mortal to exist."

I gulped.

"To correct Vine's failure as an angel, he was sent here for a while to work the other side of course, to ask forgiveness and change his thinking, and yet, here we are.

Had he repented, he would have been allowed back into His graces and allowed to resume his work in Paradise, but I can smell it clearly that he not only failed to be penitent, but also has mated with you, mortal female."

I blushed furiously. *Did we have to talk about my sex life?*

Wyrmwood blinked, breathing deeply, "Do you smell that, Brethren? Why you were a virgin!" he almost yelled, his voice like low, rumbling, deep thunder that made my bones ache with the vibrations.

I blushed again as my friends looked at me with dismay and curiosity.

"And? That's not your business," I said.

Wyrmwood smiled, "But it is. Your suffering is sweet to me. It is beginning to dawn on you that by being his lover and by loving him in return, you have doomed him to eternal suffering. How delicious that is."

Virgil looked ready to fight, "It was my choice. It was worth it to me to know the love of Alice. What we share...these precious moments will give me succor for eternity. You have nothing from your trysts. Either let us by or battle. It's no matter to me as I have never felt more powerful."

Wyrmwood blinked with hesitation. Azael flinched a little. Beelzebub looked worried. None of them would fight.

We gathered in a boat to cross the River, as Virgil steadied me since my legs trembled like gelatin. No one said anything, and I knew they were mulling over what they heard, imagining what it must have felt like to be me. I couldn't have told them since I was also in shock. Fallen angels. Virgil was Vine, and he couldn't go back to my world. How unreasonable was all of this?

Truly this was hell.

Danny finally spoke as they rowed, "Well, now you know who we are exactly and why we were sent. It was our second chance."

"What is your name really?"

"Dantanian. I was too prideful of my beauty and needed to learn modesty. I hope I am learning it."

Coral tilted his head, "The eye of a fallen angel was very valuable, I would suppose." That was a very acute observation. It made me feel sad again that he had given his own eye.

"It was. I was able to buy many potions and tokens to help us. It was all I could think to barter with."

As they left the boat, Danny pointed to stalls along the road.

At the first were bottles of potions, and the name of the stall was Uglification where they sold acids to ruin the skin, fat clothing (clothes with padding in the belly and thighs), and potions to cause rashes and pimples and hair matting.

There was a stall called Derision, where one could find sacrilegious books and shirts and materials that made fun of every race, culture, and handicap and a stall called Over Ambition.Distraction, the last shop, sold little pins and piercings that would cause pain and greatly distract the wearer. The seller sold eye-lid holders, bottles of eye-specks, sinus blockers, and potions that guaranteed headaches.

Along streets that wound off the main road were more stalls, each one offering something negative. In another stall were paintings and prints, mostly of serial killers and long dead dictators.

"If *BBDU* is in charge, then why doesn't he set the sufferers free to run around? Why are they really punished? Is he not pleased with what the bad guys did?" Dana asked.

"It's tricky. *BBDU* controls what is left to him after certain punishments and trials are set into place. People think *BBDU* has free reign and gets to run about having fun, but it isn't that at all. He rules the leftovers, the morsels dropped from the cake," Virgil said, "and the suffering is very tasty to him; he enjoys cries of pain and the wails of misery. That is his music."

I was curious about that since Danny had veered us off course to show us something. It was laid out like a giant park; paths wound about among leafless, gnarly-looking trees with benches along the way. Concrete containers were set every foot or so along the way, no more than two and a half feet long and were buried into the ground, surrounded with more concrete and with edges like a in ground pool in a backyard, only tiny.

Each pool was no more than five feet deep, and in each was a venomous mixture of boiling blood, feces, and some sort of hot lava or thick red fluid. A person was immersed into this terrible concoction to his chin, nose, or higher, depending on his crimes against property and persons. A plaque was posted to tell others who each person in the pool was.

Alexander the Great was there, and so was Attila the Hun. There was a whole section of German scientists, some Roman and Greek leaders, and some I recognized from my time: a cannibal, a child rapist, a wife/ unborn child killer.

When we returned to the road, Limmerfer was there to greet us, and Virgil grabbed him up at once since the poor cat was covered from whiskers to tail in thick blood as if he had bathed in it. He looked horrible.

"Oh, no," Cassie cried as she and Dinah watched with fear. Dinah burst into tears.

"How is he?" Coral asked, "is it bad?"

Virgil finally grinned, "Why not a drop of it is his. He is absolutely unharmed and in good health. I think this must be from whomever he fought. I guess he won."

Ignoring the blood, Dinah grabbed him into her arms and covered him with hugs and kisses. He allowed the attention.

We stopped at a stall to buy water so we could wash the cat; he didn't mind at all being scrubbed and rinsed until he was grey and white again instead of bright scarlet.

We decided to eat at the stall since there was a seating area inside the stall, looked clean, and smelled good. Danny suggested eating turtle soup and bought a huge amount of the soup and bread, and I am here to say I have never eaten turtle and was very put off by the idea.

An alternative was mock turtle soup which was, Danny explained, a rich stew made with a calf's head and brains with vegetables and a wine broth and served with forcemeat, or balls of the fat.

I went with the regular turtle soup, which was served with boiled eggs and spinach, a popular food in hell, I was told, because people seemed to hate it. Brussels sprouts, asparagus, and liver were also abundant here, but I loved the vegetables and was slightly okay with liver.

Anyway, the soup was actually delicious, and I enjoyed it.

When we left that area and entered another, we saw a chimera, a young one, in fact, who lounged in the sunlight. We were prepared to fight as we were told he was ferocious even if he were not fully grown. Instead, he only watched us and essentially backed away, his eyes fearful.

He had two heads, one of a goat and one of a lion, a goat's body, and the tail of a serpent, but the creature acted fearful of us. I saw that on each of its two faces were deep, bloody scratches, and the goat head had a flayed open cheek that still dripped blood.

"Limmy, did you do *that*?" I asked.

Limmerfer gave the beast a disinterested glance and walked past it, and we followed. The chimera trembled as it watched Limmy. How interesting that our cat had bested this monster in a battle; I wished we had been able to see the chimera getting his ass beaten, but it was done. We took turns carrying Limmerfer since he was our hero and deserved some attention.

CHapter TWeNty-NiNe: MiddLe RiNg

It was our intention to circle around the middle ring and inner ring of hell and go to the eighth where we would find the girl, get her out of prison, and end our journey. The path was frequently laced with thorny bushes that we had to carefully push away and scramble past. When we came to an opening, Limmerfer's fur stood on end, and he ran to the center to stand close to Cassie and Dinah as if protecting them.

We heard growling.

Wild, huge dogs leapt from the bushes and attacked us. One, which was my adversary, kept trying to get my arm in his jaws to bring me to the ground so he could maul my throat and finish me off. I kicked him in his face, but he didn't back away. I pulled my sword but was hit from behind as a weight caught me across my back and knocked me to the ground. Two dogs growled at me.

I dropped my sword and went for a knife I carried, bringing it up just as one of the dogs came at me; the blade slipped into his jaw and out the back of his head. My hand was in his mouth, but he didn't bite down. He pulled away, taking my knife with him and fell, twitching onto the ground.

The second dog caught my arm in his massive jaws and bit down, holding me. He would be on my neck in mere seconds, but I rolled, taking the dog with me. On all fours, with the animal attached to my arm and foaming my blood, I took my sword, slid it beneath his stomach sideways, and caught the dog in his gut. He tried to get away, but I got to my feet and unmercifully gutted him like a deer, letting blood and intestines leak everywhere.

He whined, but I didn't care. All around, my friends were fighting one or two dogs at a time, protecting Cassie, Limmerfer, and Dinah. Cassie and Limmerfer both did what they could to fend off a piebald mastiff that snapped at Dinah.

Limmerfer scratched deeply at soft noses and jumped back before the dog could bit him. He was no match for the beast, and Cassie slapped at it but was also helpless. Dinah shrieked.

I heard a loud moan that was probably meant to be a scream, but it turned into a gurgling, wet noise. Pax was on his back, and two of the dogs bit at him. One had his muzzle buried in Pax's throat.

"No. No. No," I yelled, slamming my sword down on the dog's head. I spun and ran it through the dog's thick chest and saw the animal sag and drop on top of Pax. The other dog lunged at me in retaliation, and I gutted it as well. Cassie dropped down to hold a cloth to Pax's throat, leaving Dinah to fight the other dog.

That was because there was nothing Cassie could do. It was too late to save Dinah, too.

The piebald dog had Dinah in his jaw, waving her like a rag doll. Limmerfer had his claws dug in and rode the dog angrily, hissing and swiping, but despite the deep scratches and blood, the dog didn't drop Dinah.

"Hey, come after me," I screamed at the piebald dog, "come on." I had to try to save Dinah and Limmerfer.

The bad dog jerked his head, flinging Dinah to the ground. His lips pulled back from big, bloody teeth as he growled and snarled at me, taking small steps. Limmerfer jumped free.As the dog leaped, I rolled with him, leaving my back open as he landed and spun, but I spun as well in a strong flying back kick that left me facing the dog again.

The next time he leaped, although it was hard to manage, I met his belly with my sword, ripping him open from chest to anus; then, I had to roll sideways to keep the mess of his insides from falling all over me.

The battle was about over now.

Dana and Cory were bloodied from their own wounds and from killing. Coral was the least injured and had half dozen kills around him. Danny and Virgil were almost unscathed and had killed a dozen between themselves.

I went to Cassie who tended Pax, "How is he?"

She shook her head sadly, "Not good, Alice."

"He's not…I mean…."

She nodded, tears on her greenish face, "say good bye."

"Hey, Pax," I knelt in blood and dirt, "You did good, my friend." My throat ached with the pain of sadness and sorrow. I couldn't let him go. Not Pax. I felt tears running down my face and made funny sounds when I breathed.

He couldn't speak as blood bubbled from the rips and tears on his neck, but he gave me a little smile. He pointed to me, made a motion that looked like he was saying to go on with the mission, and then he made a fist. Kick ass, he seemed to say.

"You bet. I'll get this done for sure. Thanks for your help."

He made a seesaw of his hand.

"No, you did great. We were outnumbered," Coral said.

"I love you, Pax."

He touched his heart to tell us he loved us, too.

Dana wailed loudly, letting her emotions go.

Everyone came to stand close to Pax, pat his shoulder, and say a few things. He listened and smiled, but his eyes filled with tears. In a few minutes, he stopped responding to us, and his eyes went dull; he was gone. Danny knew there was a bubbling liquid fire a few yards away off the road, and they took Pax's body to set it in there so that so he would burn away and not be eaten by animals.

We also put Dinah's little body into the fire. Cassie cried terribly hard for the child. I felt we had lost special people; it left holes in our group. It left holes in my heart.

We wanted respect for their remains but knew that was only an empty shell. Danny said Pax would be reborn on earth and have a new chance. That was good and fair, but it also made me very sad because I would never know Pax now. I felt bittersweet about that part. He said Dinah was gone. Just gone. It made me queasy to try to understand that, and Virgil said we were simply not capable of understanding the nothingness of which they spoke, and that was normal.

Death often was fine for the ones dying, but was awful for those of us left behind to mourn. I cried a long time, and so did Dana and Cassie. The men wiped their eyes often and pretended it was fumes of sulfur that bothered their eyes and made them water. I knew better. Even Limmerfer meowed sadly.

Chapter Thirty: The Inner Circle

We continued our journey with tears in our eyes for Pax and Dinah. I had lost three friends down here.

We were circling around, but when we were a little higher on the ground, we saw the inner ring and the rocks that periodically fell from the skies. I guess at times the rocks hit homes or people.

The prison was a tall, boring, concrete building with few guards (those who were guards were hideous demons) because there was no outside area. Prisoners were locked in six-foot by six-foot cells with a bed, a toilet, sink, and little else. There was no outside time or activities, and twice every day, the prisoners had meals pushed into the cells.

Danny went to the window to give the guard his paperwork and information. The demon, with the ugly yellow horns and a shiny snout, read everything three times and asked many questions in a low, bored voice. He motioned us over to a section of building with a strange design. I couldn't figure out why the side of the building contained only a large, star-shaped spot.

In a few minutes, we saw the oddest thing. A head emerged, as if a baby were being born. Then with a gigantic push, an entire person came out of the star-shaped area that opened up.

"It's a gigantic Demon's butt. He excreted her. Here, at the prison, the guilty are literally pooped out." Danny told the woman to get up, and he directed her to a spring not far away, which the guard had told him about. For a few coins, the woman was able to bathe away the waste with strong soap and cold water. She washed for a very long time, scrubbing herself, soaping and rinsing over and over.

We introduced ourselves, and she said her name was Ellie.

"Sorry, it took so long to come get you," Danny said.

"Every day is a micro second because it's forever, but every day is like a billion years because there is no end," Ellie said enigmatically.

"We did the best we could in getting here. It was difficult, and several good people lost their lives," Virgil said. He was a little angry that she didn't even bother to thank us.

"You did it to save the world, not to save me," Ellie yawned, "I was the one who was put here unfairly, and I was the one who had to suffer. Would you want to be crapped out? Do you want to be in a little cell? I was short-changed."

"Well, you are out now, so be glad," Dana said.

Before we went to the safe house where we would sleep, Danny wanted us to visit a trial being held for a prisoner. Gargoyles covered the outside of the building and were shown as statues inside as well. We walked across the marble floor and into the courtroom that looked like those I had seen on television. A jury was composed of demons, humans, hybrids, and changelings, and they had note pads that they scribbled on furiously.

The judge looked faintly familiar and was covered by a huge, curled, grey wig. I finally figured out it was a popular music star I had sometimes listened to.

Judge Mickey bellowed, "Give your evidence, and give it fast, or I'll have your head chopped off. I don't care if you are nervous or anxious, give your testimony."

The human raised his skinny arms, pleading for mercy, "But I wasn't there, and I don't have evidence to give. I know nothing."

"You admit you are stupid?"

"Well, no…I'm not stupid…."

"Then answer the question," the judge yelled.

The man again said he knew nothing, wasn't at the scene of the crime, and couldn't.

He was asked to give his opinion of the case. He claimed he had no opinion and didn't know what to say, "I only know what I have heard."

"Ah. The witness admits he has heard information. Give the court your testimony. What did you hear?"

"I heard that the accused, John, was found praying and carrying a hand made cross and was arrested for public indecency and heresy."

"Make note of that, jurors. He had heard that. Having heard such, it must be true." The judge slammed his gavel down, and an attendant slammed a hammer down onto the human's head. When the witness slumped, he was dragged from the courtroom.

The next witness claimed to know John and said she had never seen or heard John pray and had never seen him carry a cross.

"Have you ever asked him if he did either?" the judge demanded.

"No, your Honor," the woman said.

"Then, you show a laxness I don't like. *The lax, Their shoes do clack, When they hurry away, to avoid work to be done, and so are beheaded by Max.*"

The attendant, obviously Max, grinned happily and nodded.

"Can you say he did not engage in these behaviors?" the judge asked.

"I can't say either way," the woman said.

"You *can't?*"

"I could if I knew, but I don't know, and, therefore, I can't say."

The judge glared, "You are very obstinate. I would rap a ditty about that but have no words to fit *obstinate,* and I have said it; it is recorded; I am stuck with it. Bother. I find this witness engaging in behavior that inhibits my creativity. Throw her into the prison."

The next witness also got into trouble as it had a ratty-looking head and whiskers that were too long. Nothing made sense here, and everyone seemed to be doomed, but it was an interesting event to see.

Imagine my shock when they called the next witness.

"We call Alice," Max said, looking right at me.

"What do you know of this?" the judge asked me.

"Nothing."

"Nothing at all?"

"I am new here and traveling through. I don't know anything of this or anyone involved as I wasn't here."

"That's important," said the judge, "s*he isn't involved, and she wants it resolved, the case of John, The heresy he wrought, She wishes to be absolved.*"

"I wasn't even here; that much is clear; these are the facts. This is the truth; I am innocent, I do fear." I tried to make sense, but thought I was less than clever in my rhyming. We all waited for several seconds while the judge considered my response.

"She is innocent. Next witness!"

While the time was good, we left the courtroom and never knew what became of the other witnesses or the accused, John. I knew Danny had taken us there to hear the insane court proceedings so that we would better understand how everything worked here in hell. What the lesson would help me with later, I didn't know, but Danny thought it important.

I knew that I was missing a part of this crazy puzzle and didn't know how I could find the piece and place it.

The house where we were to stay was large with gardens and a forest at the edge of the lawn. It was one of the most inviting places we had seen, and we were told that it was an expensive get-away home for those who had the money. Danny said the owner owed him a favor, and this was how Danny collected.

Coral set about making a meal: lamb and thin bread with onions, peppers and a cucumber sauce that I thought was Greek, a chicken and noodle soup with slices of zucchini, cracked black pepper, and something like cilantro. The other dish, a salad, was of olives, tomatoes, cheese, and cucumbers over spinach. It all smelled and looked delicious, and only Coral could take the simplest of ingredients and make such a wonderful dinner.

A pair of very pale demonesses took our clothing and handed us soft pants and shirts to wear while our clothes were cleaned. We each had a bath as well, but this was a new experience. We had a whole army of attendants.

First, my attendant waited for me to undress, and then she rubbed an oil-scented and lemony herb into my skin, and I sat for a few minutes in a steam room where rocks and water heated up to mist the room. While I stood sweating, she used wooden implements to scrape away the oil and accumulated oil. Once I lay down, she rubbed my skin hard and with long strokes and explained she was getting the deepest dirt out of my pores.

After that, my attendant settled me into a hot bath and used salt and a rough brush to scrub my skin clean. She also shampooed my hair, rubbed conditioner into it, and then rinsed it. My hair smelled like lavender. While I soaked, she towel dried my hair, brushing and blotting each strand until it gleamed.

When I was out of the water, I lay on a soft table, and my attendant rubbed my sore muscles and blotted salve into scratches and on my injured arm before she gently bandaged it. My soreness began to vanish as she rubbed the muscles, oxygenating them and relieving the pain.

I dozed.

I slept for an hour, she said, and I felt fully revived but still relaxed. When I walked out barefoot to the commons area, my friends looked equally as relaxed. I felt a pang of sadness for the loss of Dinah, Pax, and Annie.

"Almost time to eat," Coral said, "you look like you feel better."

"I do. I finally feel clean."

"Go find the rest for me? We'll eat when everyone is here."

I went to look for the others; the food smelled good, and I was starving. Cory fell into step with me, and we found Danny busily looking over maps, but he said he would come eat. Cassie was in the garden, her face sad, but she perked up when we said the meal was ready. We looked everywhere for Virgil and Dana and found them in the last room.

Chapter Thirty-One: Mirror Images

As the door opened, I gasped.

Dana was tall, with an Amazonian body, strong and powerful. Her body shined with the oil from her massage, and she was nude. Virgil, his body like a Greek sculpture, was also nude, and he held her to him. Ignoring us after a quick look to see who had arrived, Virgil pressed himself to Dana, kissing her like a starving man, groaning and rubbing her back with one hand. Her hands roamed all over his muscles.

Cory and I stood in the doorway, unable to look away as Vigil lifted Dana, sat her on a table, and entered her with one fast move. She let out a shrill scream of pleasure. He kissed her breasts, and she wiggled in excitement.

How could he cheat on me? How could she do this to me? I felt stabbed with jealousy, betrayal, and pain.

Cory pushed me away and yelled at them, one obscenity after another, but they didn't stop.

"Why are you yelling?" Virgil stood beside us in the hall, looking confused.

"Virg?" I asked, "What? How? Who is…?"

Cory pushed past us and looked into the room, "Get out. We've no time for your mischief." Picking up a vase of flowers on a small table, he threw it at the couple, hitting Dana full on in her face; her nose began to pour blood. Both faced Virgil.

"I could have mated your woman, Vine," the other Virgil said.

"True. And know if you touch her, I will spend the rest of my days torturing you for the impunity. This I give my word to."

Looking at the false Virgil, I saw he looked differently, as did the false Dana. I couldn't figure out what was different, but there was something.

"Mirrored images," Cory whispered. He had figured it out. He grabbed a paperweight and flung it at the one mirror in the room, shattering it into a million, glittering shards. Both false beings screamed and looked suddenly flat before they, too, broke into small pieces and winked away. It was as if they had never been there.

Virgil looked into my face, saw I was okay, and gathered me into his arms, "I can't imagine what you must have thought. I am so sorry."

"It wasn't you. It was them...tricking me. How evil that was," I said.

"Some enjoy playing games. We all have evil mirror twins but never have to be around them, of course. Here, you see few mirrors because the twins can roam when one has them, and even the most vile demons resent their twins impersonating them."

Dana and Coral looked anxious as we went to the commons room, but we explained quickly, and Dana turned pale.

"I would never do that," she said.

"I know, but it was right before my eyes," I told her.

Despite that horrible event, we ate well and relaxed again after a search of the house that revealed no more mirrors. Danny warned us never to trust a mirror. Our twins all lived on the other side where there was no heaven or hell or worlds, but one place where things were very backwards and where many people were very evil and sadistic. It was a land ruled by the Red Queen, a terrible woman who enjoyed chaos more than anything.

"If you, in your world, see a hurricane or tornado, a house fire, a useless, destructive event, you can be sure the Red Queen had a hand in it."

"What a bitch," Dana mused.

I retired early with Virgil sharing my bed, and he spent a half an hour telling me over and over that the mirrored Virgil was sick and that the real Virgil, the one with me, would never do anything so horrible.He said that I was the woman he had loved enough to be punished for. He was devastated that I had witnessed such a terrible thing and had every reason to think it was he.

I kissed him and said I understood it was a cruel trick, but he remained upset. As I watched him, I traced his muscles with my fingertips, noting how perfectly he was built. I had once thought him plain, but he was like a Greek god, unbelievably handsome. His blue eyes were like the colors of the seas, light colored and expressive, changing with the tides, deepening and darkening when he was worried.

He slid a beautiful silver ring that he had been wearing onto my left hand's ring finger. It magically fit me as he did. He looked into my face with his fathomless blue eyes, asking a million questions with just one look. I hugged him and kissed his whole face, I would wear the ring.

αγάπη μου όλη την αιωνιότητα was engraved into the silver band. *"My love all eternity,"* he said. He had worn the ring to remind him of me and that he had loved me even before he had known me. I want you to have it, to know I love you beyond worlds."

Not just eternity, it said, but *all* eternity. Not just love, but *all*.

"What did those demons mean? By being with me physically, what did that matter?" I asked, "Why did they care I was a virgin?"

Virgil stared at the ceiling as he spoke, "I broke rules. I was not allowed that. After this mission, I could have returned to heaven, as long as I let you go in my heart and mind, but I knew I couldn't and didn't want to either, so by making love to a mortal, I have doomed myself to remain here forever. And moreover, I took a virgin."

"Virgil…why? No, that isn't…."

"Alice, I made a choice. I would rather be here and have these moments and have the memories than to go back there and have the memories taken away as if I had never known you. No. I won't let you leave my heart and soul. My choice and I made it."

"I love you. I don't want to…." I began weeping in great whooping sobs, "I can't leave you here when I finish this and have to go back."

"And you can't stay, and I can't leave. Alice, there is nothing we can do, but there is right now."

He kissed me, and in time, I enjoyed his attentions, stopped crying, and later, slept, but I didn't stop thinking about there had to be a way to work this out. *There just had to be.*

CHapter THirty-TWo: A HeLLuVa PLace to Be

The next area, Danny told us, would test our mettle; everything up to this point had been in preparation for this next trial as it would be emotionally daunting.

I took that to mean we would see some freaky things and have our brains seriously messed with. I'm not complaining, but this constant horror and fear could cause deep depression, and I felt a little tired of the misery, which is strange, because you know the people sentenced to hell were seriously tired of it.

My heart went out to poor Cassie who was stuck here as a worm.

Malebodge was the name of the next area, and it was impossible to skirt around even if we had wished to because the road led to our ultimate goal. Many roads led to the center since it was the main section of hell where *Big Boss Down Under* lived. Danny said overhead it would look like a wheel with spokes.

As we talked, an airplane flew across the hazy sky. In a few seconds, it seemed to pause, but then, it fell wing over wing, plowing into the ground some distance away and erupting in a fiery explosion that we felt in even in our feet.

Every few days, the plane would fill up with people and then would have mechanical problems, so the passengers screamed and cried a few minutes before they plunged to the earth to burn alive again.

"Plane-watching" was a favorite activity of some in hell, and many raced over to crash sites to see, smell, and hear the abject misery of those who were broken to pieces, ripped apart, or burned.

"That's sickening even for hell. Why would anyone want to look?"

"People watch *Faces of Death* in your world, Alice. Curiosity, or a reminder that no matter what, they are better off than those poor boogers, I think, makes us feel glad it isn't us, and many like to know what it looks like…." Danny said.

Virgil held my hand as we entered the area and looked at the Bolgias. The first area was brutal as pimps and seducers walked in opposite lines, back and forth, while demonic guards whipped their backs, arms, and legs.

One line was being punished because there had been liaisons between customers and sexual outlets, pimps, and madams and men in expensive slacks or women in fancy skirts. Prisoners of the other line were dressed in skimpy shirts, shorts, or tight pants and were call girls, whores, or prostitutes.

The demons whipped their prisoners' backs into bloody, tattered strips that hung like festooned decorations along their waists. Although the people often fell, they had to scramble back to their feet or be kicked and dragged along.

Flesh healed only to be slashed open again. Danny told us the guards had six-hour shifts each so that the torture went on around the clock.

The lines of the beaten people stretched as far as the eye could see.

Another part was even worse.It was as if someone had set up rows of aquariums, deposited people inside, and filled the aquariums with feces.

I was so glad we couldn't smell that. Even though the people had been there for ages, they still vomited as the wafting scent enveloped them, and Danny said they added fresh feces often and experimented to find the worst textures and smells possible.

"What did they do?" Dana asked as she wondered about a man who was buried to his chin.

"They have gifts of speech: one group of people, who used words in speech or writing to hurt in order to gain something, are punished here. Their words were crap, and so they are living in crap."

She wrinkled her nose at Danny, "That's awful. Isn't that the comedian who always made fun of people with cruel, snide remarks?"

"It is."

Dana nodded, "Makes sense, I guess. Yuk."

"You can also find those who used their gift of speech to use flattery to trick people. There are those who promised women great film careers but instead got them hooked on drugs and put them in porn films.

You also might find ones who lied to children, saying they were looking for lost puppies or had ice cream, but kidnapped the children instead."

"That's horrible, too," I said.

"They used flattery and clever words, like Satan himself, to get what they wanted:power or money."

"It sounds like they got what they deserved," Coral muttered.

"Next are the Halls of Simony."

"Who?"

Danny laughed, "Not who but what. Simony means paying for religious offices."

On the ceiling were blocks of stone, and between each pair was a human's head, held into place by large vises.

They were so tight that a person was left hanging a few feet above the ground by the stone, and each had trickles of blood, which ran from where their ears were being mashed and torn by the blocks of stone all the way to the ground.

They were lined up in rows that looked as if they went on forever but made an enormous circle, actually, and had roads like the one we were on, dissecting the large circles.

As the victims hanged from the ceiling, the victim's feet were above pits of fire that were fed coal by workers. Flames licked up to bare feet to blister, burn, and char tender toes and soles.

Although many kicked and tried to draw their legs way from the heat, there was no escape, and their feet eternally burned.

"Now I get *'holding one's feet to the fire'* as a phrase," Cory muttered.

"Religious offices should be given to those who are called to serve and can best serve and care for their parishioners. Buying positions to gain more power and money while doing evil deeds is evil," Virgil told us.

Wails and screams for mercy made my head throb.

The next area featured people called False Prophets. They suffered, having their heads turned and twisted cruelly because in their time alive, they had engaged in twisted, false information in order to procure money from followers. Some astrologers were there, along with sorcerers, and many fake faith healers, as well."They lied to people and gave them false predictions, false hopes, and misled them in order to get rich. That's nasty to promise people cures for maladies and tell them to throw away their medicine and then they take their money," Coral said.

Danny showed us the next tableau: corrupt politicians immersed in a pool of boiling tar. They were stuck in the tar, and the more they were caught in their own lies and deceit in the real world, the more they struggled in the tar, never to be free.

He said, "All they get to eat is tar. They were supposed to have helped people, but instead, they grew fat and rich and only cared for themselves, so for their evil mouths and fat bellies, they get hot tar."

Wild Hog, Dog Scratcher, and Curly Beard were among the twelve beasts that guarded the *tar babies*. Each was gnarled, black of skin, horned, and winged; fungus grew on their skin.

Among the people in that pool of boiling tar, I recognized a few high-ranking females who still had bad hair styles and make up disasters and continued to be the *fashion police's* worst nightmare; a congressman who smiled a lot while he lied through his teeth; and a self-educated, tall, thin man, who was known to wear a fancy top hat and once held a very high office. Along with these, I noticed Asian rulers, several dictators from South American and Middle Eastern countries, and a mean-spirited Frenchman; all struggled to get out.A big man, still smoking a cigar and now out of his well-known tomb, flayed in the tar, along with so many others that I lost count. Each was gnarled; blistered--sticky black skin; horned; and winged; fungus grew on their skin.

Malacoda was the leader of the Malebranche guards; his name meant Evil Tail. Periodically, one would use a sharp claw or a tail to press the politicians deeper into the boiling tar, sometimes sending them in to suffocate.

When a politician wailed and cried for mercy, the Malebranche howled in guttural laughter, rumbling malevolently.

When one of the devils, Farfafello, or Goblin, as he was called, came too close, sniffling at us, Virgil would swing his sword into the creature with a thunderous force, sending Farfarello into the air and into the edge of the tar pit.

As we left that area, one of the devils climbed from the tar, whining and mewling, to the amusement of the other devils.

They could have attacked us, but they were a little frightened of the two angels with us. Even fallen angels carried a certain position in hell.

The next area looked normal, or as normal as one could find in hell. There were stalls, small houses, buildings, a few parks, and dying trees.

I saw the usual demoness mothers with reptilian children, demons busy along the street, human and demon prostitutes and pimps.

The School of Morbid Learning was the place where the students were taught to glorify Hitler's crimes and beliefs, make flesh-eating bacteria and bombs, write obscene poetry, and sing songs about the humor of the carnage of September 11. During recess, the human and beast teachers walked and played with children.

A fire station made me wonder what happened there until Danny said that periodically the fire crew got a call, and the firemen drove to a house where they sprayed it with fire hoses until the building was properly engulfed in flames.

After that explanation, I could guess what the police at the police station did.

As we passed various restaurants, I gagged and shivered at the fare they offered. Essel's Pepper Palace had a little sign that read: *'Try our habenero to raise you temperature and blood pressure.*Puppy Palace assuredly didn't sell pet treats.

And Limmerfer hissed at the Puppy Palace unhappily. He had dog friends back at home.

Danny pointed."Fly in My Soup is a popular place, too, and you would not believe the things they set afloat on top of the soups. Rat droppings and other ripe-smelling items were grated, as Parmesan cheese would be, atop creamy potato soup. It was seriously disgusting."

In a window, we saw an intestinal crank. The shop was called Lilith's Spanish Spider since she was like a black widow that wove webs of torture. We could see an array of devices meant for torture that people could buy for *fun*.

"Why?" was all Dana would say, her eyes wide with wonder. "What kinds of nuts think up these places?"

Saul's Brimstone and Assorted Fineries sat nestled between Beth's Baby Bludgeoning Boutique and Scotty's Pre-Sanded Toilet-Paper Emporium (*'your ring of fire'*). Dan's Funeral Home was on a corner and claimed to both *'stab 'em and slab 'em.*

"I think horror fiction writers own some of these shops," Danny said, "Look. Cracked Spine Books: they break them, you buy them, but do you know what the book spines are made of? Or the paper? Or the ink? Exactly. Sick, huh?

Over there, see the smoke boiling out into the sky? Gary's Baby Oil Refinery. They say he doesn't always produce a pure product but adds all kinds of other oils and junk into his wares, and that's the best they *say*," Danny added.

"This place should be burned to ashes, Danny. It's an affront to decency," Coral said.

"Yes, it is. Satan makes sure it stays repugnant and offensive. Imagine the energy this place uses in keeping up the revulsion. Hatred alone keeps the lights burning here." Danny pointed out the Department of Racism and Bashing that he said conducted enough power, alone, to run the Infernal Subway.

"I wish our mission was to burn this place away," I said.

Nothing much looked differently here than where we arrived days ago, but this was supposed to be a worse area where people suffered more. Except for everyone seeming slower, as if he were walking underwater and sweating badly, there didn't seemed to be anything odd.

"So what's the deal?" Cory asked. He noticed the same.

"These are hypocrites who live here," Virgil explained. "Watch how they move."

"Slowly. They sweat a lot, too," Cassie wrinkled her nose.

"All clothing here is infused and lined with lead, a lot of lead. Lead in hats, shirts, dresses, pants, underwear; everything has the extra weight even socks and shoes.

They are weighted down by their hypocrisy; they each carry more weight as time goes on until those who have been here a very long time can no longer move." Virgil pointed to what I thought were life-like statues of humans with a Roman-demon look. They sat in hunched-over positions.

"And why don't they just refuse clothing and go naked?" Coral asked.

We walked a little more, and finally Danny found someone he was looking for: a prostitute who wore a tube top and very short shorts; we could see a lot of her. Threaded deeply through her skin were lead safety pins, or the like, but they were soldered closed so they could not be removed. These added weight.

"She must have tried that, to go naked, but the *Legions of Lead* found out and made sure she was weighted down. They get no second chances here," Danny told us.

He pointed out another example. A woman had lead pellets inserted and stitched into her collarbone area and around her ankles and up her shins. It looked as if tiny things lived under her skin.

We learned that these, the hypocrites, were weighted down by false faces and false words and so were weighed down as their punishments. Everyone in this area was always tired and struggled to get around with the lead holding each back.

"Poetic justice," I said.

I had listened to my father talk about how criminals and evil people never got what they deserved, that prisons were too easy, and so was the death penalty. He always said criminals should have to face the same types of misery comparable to their crimes. Dad had no sympathy for people who harmed others, stole, or lied.

I knew that people did, in fact, face horrible, just punishments for their crimes. I wondered how Dad would feel knowing how long criminals suffered and how badly.

To be honest, I cared, but I didn't care; I was ready to stop seeing this. It was one thing to judge and wish bad things on people but another to see it happening. Of course, I wouldn't mind seeing people suffer a little for what they had done to my friends. I would gladly kill those dogs over and over.

"I think this is stupid. Could anyone not think of a better punishment than lead clothing? What a joke," Ellie said, "being in the prison was far worse."

"It seems bad to me having to carry all that weight," Coral said.

"Really? I think it's a joke."

"Not to them," I told Ellie.

She giggled, "They look weird moving all slow." She mimicked their movements.

"I haven't seen anything *funny in hell* yet. Even if they deserve it, I don't enjoy seeing torture," I said.

"Have you seen lice-hookers? They are funny. So is the Duchess," Ellie said.

"I didn't find them humorous, and the Duchess is vile, not funny," Coral argued.

"Really? Her suckling-pig baby?" Ellie smacked her lips.

I gave her a dirty look.

"Now, this area here gets a little better or at least more fun and exciting," Ellie said.

"We don't have time for *The Game*," Danny told her.

Another tableaux had a demonic guard glared angrily at us; he stood with several other guards; all of them were yellow-white like dreadful larvae. Rolls of fat covered their bodies, dark horns sat on their heads, and long, curved wickedly sharp claws motioned to us.

Glancing at Danny and Virgil, I wondered if we were about to fight these guards and was worried because they looked dangerous and because several dozen were around the area.

The guard who spoke to us pointed, *"You are almost late."*

"We're travelers...." began Danny.

"I don't give a rat's ass who or what you are. It's time for the show, and in case you are unaware, the *Obscenity Act of 1998* requires everyone to attend. That means travelers, too."

"Okay, where do we go?"

The demon showed Danny as he pointed out a building that looked like a Roman coliseum. That didn't seem like a good omen.

As we found seats on the wooden benches, attendants sold bugs in a bag and other nauseating snacks so the place, Cassie told us, smelled like vomit and wet earth.

When the show began, Ellie explained it with excitement that unsettled me, "Now see there? Those are like centaurs, but as you, no doubt, have noticed, they are a little different."

I thought centaurs to be semi-attractive men with the bodies of horses in mythology and very good with the bow and arrows. Their faces were hideous since their noses and lips were enormous and eyes tiny. Their human skin from the waist up was maggot-white, soft, and hairless. A milky white fluid oozed out as sweat.

Their lower bodies were those of horses, but not well-muscled, pretty horses, more of what a small child would form from clay. The mane wasn't shiny, the muscles were wrong, and the legs were comically long and fat. Big green and brown snakes wound from their ribs to writhe in the air as capes or weird wings.

"Cool. Huh?" Ellie said.

The centaurs announced the game and welcomed everyone.

I saw about half the crowd looked unhappy to be at The Game and miserable already while the other half was excited to be at The Game, cheering and shouting.

In a few minutes, a group of thieves was ushered into the middle of the building. Their faces showed terror, and no matter why there were here, I felt badly for whatever they were to about to face. Would it be lions? Or worse?

"Now watch this," Ellie said.

The thieves, a few men and two women, glanced at the next door that cranked open and then began running around the ring as fast as they could.

From the open doorway, several giant scorpions raced out, followed by fast running lizards with teeth like sharks. Various snakes and smaller reptiles followed the large beasts. The creatures hissed and squealed with blood lust and the thrill of the chase.

All who were running began to scream, but they had no weapons or protection.

Within seconds, a man became cornered, and one of the scorpions stung him, but before the big lizards could eat him, his body started changing. His legs drew into his body, he fell to the ground on all fours, and a tail sprouted from his rear that grew long and shiny. His head bulged and twisted as he screamed with pain until he looked somewhat like a scorpion. His tail lengthened and curled up where a barb formed. His body segmented, and suddenly he was free to chase the rest of the thieves.

A lizard bit a woman's hand off, and within a minute, her body changed, becoming greenish, wart-covered, and lizard-fish like; then, she too was on the hunt.

As each metamorphosed, he would twist and scream with the pain, rolling around and begging for help. The change was horrific, and I could not imagine the mental turmoil of such a thing. As soon as those were changed, the next group of thieves was released from a doorway to run around the stadium while onlookers cheered and groaned as bets were lost and won.

"They stole when they were alive, and so in this punishment, their lives, their humanness, and their everything were also stolen and replaced by their being a bug or lizard.

They say it is pure insanity to be the one who is punished. He turns, and then he turns back bit by bit, very slowly over a month or so and is sent back to do it again," Ellie told us. Her eyes shined with excitement and blood lust.

"Tell me you don't enjoy this?" Dana snapped at Ellie.

"Well, I have been in prison a long time. I dreamed of entertainment, being clean, good food, and a man...or a woman."

"This isn't entertainment. It's sickening. What's wrong with you?"

She didn't answer, and we sat through the rest of the show until Danny said it was okay to make our leave and not be penalized.

CHapter THirty-THree: IS NotHiNg oUt oF BoUNd?

The second that we left the show and were down the road, I furiously slammed Ellie against the side of a building. "I asked you what is wrong with you? I said. I have lost three friends down here and subjected other friends and myself to infernal misery and debasement, breathed noxious fumes, snorted demon bones, and will have nightmares the rest of my life in order to come here to save you."

"I...."

I didn't let her speak, "Tell me one reason you are worth any of that. Right now, I don't see anything particularly redeemable about you."

"She's kind of cute," Cory said.

Never turning my angry eyes from Ellie, I held one hand to my side, "Cory, shut up."

"Alice...."

Again my arm went out, "Shut up, Danny."

"I didn't ask you to come here, did I?" Ellie asked.

Okay, I had developed a bit of a temper down in Hell, which was not a nice addition to my personality, but I was really angry.

Without thinking, I popped Ellie right in her eye. There. That would swell up nicely and turn purple. She wasn't going to be cute in an hour or less. I leaned in again, "Tell me one reason you are worth this."

"You hit me."

"Yep. I'll likely hit you again."

Coral wrapped his big arms about me and carried me back several yards. He didn't let me go until Dana reported that my eyes

127

had become less glassy and I looked sane. Once I was free, I sat down on a dead tree. Everyone else sat around or stood about.

"It isn't for her. It's for your parents and the world, and it is the right thing to do.

She wasn't supposed to be here," Coral reminded me.

"Right. I get it. But I don't like her," I said.

"I don't like you, either," she told me.

Danny said we had to stop soon because he didn't want to stop in the next area.

It was way too dangerous for us. As we walked, Ellie flirted with Virgil, and I was getting close to punching her again, but he yanked her to the side, making her whine with the pain of his grip on her arm. He whispered something that sounded gruff and made her look sad; when we walked on, she no longer flirted and kept her mouth shut.

We passed several stalls. Rob's Real Roasted Ribs (BYOR) sat on one side and Gloria's Ghoulish Ghoulash on the other side, along with Delightful Asian, Fifty Blades of Flay, and Hatter's Baby Batter (sperm bank).

"Those kids born from women who use that place…horrible…big floppy ears and funny shaped heads…dumb as doornails," Danny said, "but those shops are gaining in popularity as everyone wants to help build the infernal population. It's big business."

"Is nothing out of bounds?" I asked.

Danny thought for a second, "Ummm. Not that I can think of."

Chapter Thirty-Four: Dee and Dum

Another house we visited was back in the woods a little and resembled a big, shambling haunted house with cornices and a creaky front door and loaded with what looked to be priceless antiques. I saw crystal vases, Persian rugs, inlaid mother of pearl-topped tables, velvet drapes, and more opulence than I could have dreamed of. The creepiness outside might have fit into my version of hell, but the inside was beautiful and wasn't unpleasant in any way.

"You must be rich," Ellie said rudely as we entered the home.

The hosts were twin men, tall and rather chubby, with round heads and silly looking, prissy clothing. One was Dee, and the other was Dum.

Dum giggled, "This? This is what no one else wants. Old stuff like this is very unchic. We furnished with thrown away junk no one else wanted."

They said we were *nearly late* and ushered us to a table once we had washed our hands. The huge dining table was set with china, gold flatware, and crystal goblets for water and wine. Once we were seated with linen napkins on our laps, the twins brought out so many dishes that I lost count, but the dinner was themed like Thanksgiving so we had turkey and ham, dishes of every vegetable possible, stuffing, cranberry sauce, and casseroles.

I told the brothers they were excellent cooks and the meal was perfect. I had to pause to say it, and the others were eating so fast and heavily that they couldn't get a word in between bites. We ate way too much but made room somehow for at least a few bites of the cakes and pies served for dessert, along with tea.

No wonder Dee and Dum were obscenely obese.

"So Alice," Dum asked me, "have you considered that maybe you are at home in bed, asleep, and are only dreaming all of this?"

"It would be a long dream," I said.

"Dreams occur in a split second anyway. Maybe we are a part of your dream and you'll awaken and find this never happened," Dum went on.

"I doubt that."

Dee took up the argument, "Then, maybe you are just a figment of someone's dream yourself and this is all a dream. When that person awakens, you'll cease to exist."

"So maybe this is all a nightmare, and I'll awaken at home in bed without being here? I think I'd be sorry I missed this delicious dinner," I said.

That logic didn't seem right, but wondering about it ruined my appetite, and after we cleaned up and chatted with our hosts, I went to bed with Virgil. He assured me this wasn't a dream and was real.

It was a long time before I fell asleep.

In the morning, before I could even finish eating, I was furious again; this time it was because I saw Cory and Ellie come out of a bedroom together.

"What have you done? She's supposed to be a virgin, Cory. How can we get her out?"

"I am?"

"She is?"

"Isn't she?" I asked Danny and Virgil.

Danny shook his head and backed away from me, "Ummm. That isn't a deal breaker. She wasn't when she got here, so...."

"You said you were, but it was okay if I were your first. You lied, huh?" Cory asked Ellie.

She shrugged.

"Whatever. Not like it was love anyway," he sulked.

"The Red Queen will be here soon, and she will guide you across to the next section," Dee said.

"Isn't she the bad chick from the mirror world?" Coral asked, worried.

"Oh. Yes and no. This one is the good one from here. I mean the better one...you know...."

I stared at Dee in confusion, "So it's not the mirrored, worst one."

"Right. This one is just a bit of a slut. Let me tell you what she did...."

I held a hand up, "Dee, what are you and Dum in hell for?"

He narrowed his eyes, and Dum giggled, "Gossiping. All the people in this area are here because our gossip and lies caused great discord and division: in war times or in marriages, in kingdoms, friendships; we all ruined lives because of our deeds."

Dee forgave my question to ask, "So do you want to hear what the Red Queen did?"

"No, thank you."

We cleaned up, got dressed for battle, gathered our weapons, and waited for the Red Queen. Vigil whispered that he was concerned over how on-edge I had become.

I wiped a tear and told him our quest was almost over and I would lose him. All this was for a girl who was less than likeable. I rubbed at the ring he had given me, repeating in my head that it was *all love all eternity*.

"*Ζω για σένα. Θα είναι η αγάπη. Είστε αναπνοή μου και την καρδιά μου. Είστε άπειρο,*" He told me this: I was his life, his love, his breath, and his heartbeat. *Άπειρο* was the Greek word for *infinity*. Until he translated, I didn't know what he said, but the words sounded like poetry and were beautiful when he said them.

He said, "*Για πάντα η γυναίκα μου.*" He smiled and told me that I was forever his wife, now.

The romance calmed me. His words were soothing balm to my spirit.

CHapter THirty-Five: THe Red QueeN

When the Red Queen arrived, Dum and Dee introduced us, and then they left for the *Sowers of Discord* meeting where each stood and said, "Hello, I am Dee (or whatever the name is), and I have sown discord and divided people...."

They were then hacked and sliced with a sword that a demon welded. Neither twin looked forward to his turn but had been through this time and time again and knew that they could handle the punishment to be dealt to them, would heal again, and go back through the punishment when it was their turn.

I thought it sounded dreadful.

"Come along," The Red Queen ordered. She was tall, red-haired, pale-skinned, and wore a long, fancy, royal-looking dress of scarlet and trimmed with some soft, white fur. About her throat and wrists and on her fingers were jewels set with enormous rubies.

She handed us handkerchiefs and said we had to wear them around our mouths and noses at all times as we traveled. She cautioned us not to touch anything and to avoid contact with others at all costs.

She shared a story with us. Ulysses was in the area we left before this last one because he used the Trojan horse for deception and he was a fraud. He used trickery to gain an advantage. In the next area she said Trojans punished Sinon as he had been the one to convince the Trojans to roll the horse into the walls of Troy and thus he was a liar. While it was wrong to deceive, it was worse to have actively pushed trickery.

"Who else is there?" Coral asked.

"Counterfeiters, perjurers, liars, and tricksters."

As we walked into this township, we saw thousands of pallets on the ground as far as we could see in both directions. On each was a feeble body.

Danny explained, "They were a disease on society, and they suffer diseases here that are never soothed. As you can see, there are millions. Lying spreads like a cancer."

The Red Queen and he pointed to various pallets and people. One was suffering bubonic plague with a bubo the size of a grapefruit under his arm that looked ready to burst open; the man groaned and cried with unimaginable pain and fever.Another man on a pallet scratched at a terrible rash, a woman rocked back and forth, holding her head and wailing, a teen boy screeched as tiny worms crawled from his pores, and several bled, vomited, or suffered diarrhea with hemorrhagic flu and dysentery. Every disease and ailment was here.

The Red Queen set us onto a path right down the center instead of the other side. When I asked why we were going the wrong, longer way, she shook her head, "Oh, you don't want to go forwards on that other path since it leads right into the area they keep the wolf-sick ones."

"The what?" Dana asked.

"They howl and can't take water. Their throats and necks pain them."

"Rabies," Coral said.

"They are prone to attacking any who comes near them, and they spread the sickness through their bites. Those to the right have diseases of the urine, the heart, the chest, face, and head," The Queen waved a hand, and we saw thousands lined up on pallets.

"Oh," I said.

"And to the left, we have diseases of the brain and the mentally disturbed. You see many are tied down? They can be violent, imagine images, or try to escape." She shuddered, "And there, straight ahead, we will find diseases of the skin such as boils, blisters, rashes, lesions, and peeling, so we'll take this path."

In a little while, we walked under an arch, and the Red Queen said we were in the *Valley of the Lepers*. *"I will fear no evil, thy rod and staff will beat them back. But if there be a truth in what they say, That angel-forms we cannot see, Go with us on our way;*

Then surely she is with me here, I dimly feel her spirit near--The morning-mists grow thin and clear, And Death brings in the Day."

"Or *he* for the angels." I reached to hold Virgil's hand, and he grinned at me.

The Queen quoted again, *"Hark, said the dying man and sighed, To that complaining tone--Like sprite condemned, each eventide, To walk the world alone, At sunset, when the air is still, hear it creep from yonder hill. It breathes upon me dead and chill. A moment, and is gone. My son, it reminds me of a day left half a life behind that I have prayed to put away, forever from my mind. But bitter memory will not die: It haunts my soul when none is nigh: I hear its whisper in the sigh of that complaining wind."*

I swallowed hard. All around were men and women wrapped in dirty grey bandages, gauze, and sheets. Many were covered head to toe with only their eyes showing, and others were less covered so we could see their silvery, rotting skin flaking and crumbling away. Some faces were missing noses; that were appalling. Many were absent fingers so they reached for us with some wrapped things that looked like paws.

We had to keep our distance, but I felt sympathy for the poor people.

There were stalls in one small area run by those who suffered alopecia, asthma, sleep disorders, erectile dysfunctions, and restless leg syndrome. They sold food and bandages, sheets and ointments, potions, and a variety of gemstones.

"Those with bowel and stomach diseases supply so much to the *State of Decay and Sewage Benefit* that this area stays fairly well supplied with food and medication and bandages although they never get relief and never heal."

"But they lie in the open on hard pallets," Dana said.

Ellie giggled, and I gave her a dirty look.

"Yes, they do, but this wheel branches off into the flat lands and close to one of the rivers that leads to the Styx, so their infections and waste run into the waters and keep the water filthy. But...never mind that. My point is there are millions. There is no where they could be housed, and there is no one to tend all of them," the Queen said.

She stopped at a bridge, saying she could go no farther and had done her service. She said good-bye and clutched my hand as she leaned close to whisper a warning to me. I nodded.

It was as I had suspected; Ellie was not trustworthy. The Red Queen said she felt it in her bones.

CHapter THirty-Six: BeLiaL VerSuS ViNe aNd DaNtaNiaN

We climbed upwards to reach the icy cold tops of the mountains. In the ice, we saw many frozen within a cold, hard wall, their eyes staring outwards with fear and misery. Danny said they were conscious, but encased so they couldn't move but had to stay in place with the ice frigid against their flesh. I saw Mordred, the hateful son who tried to kill his own father King Arthur but not his mother Morgana. Cain was there as well since he had killed his own brother, Able, and this was the place for those who did harm to their own family members.

Others I didn't know since they were those who harmed their own kingdoms and political parties or benefactors, and then there were those who betrayed their ultimate rulers. One person here I did recognize: Judas Iscariot. His feet stuck out from the ice while poison-filled wasps stung him.

"Get behind the trees," Danny yelled. We heard thundering footsteps approaching.

We had to scoot to the edge of the road for safety and to hide as demonic soldiers came marching through the mountain pass. Despite the powder, we could smell them: body odors, rancid sweat, and stinky feet. We were told there were 4,207 of them in all, and it took a long time for them to pass. All were hideous demons of various colors, sizes, and shapes, but all had wicked eyes and brutal glares.

"They will pass through all the areas where we've been and torture anyone they find, maim and kill at random, rape, burn, and cause them more misery. It's what they do sometimes to add a little unhappiness," Danny said.

"As if the place can stand more misery," I muttered.

"They add untold grief. Just be thankful we are hidden," Danny whispered.

It was cold as we hid behind trees and watched the demon soldiers.

"There is Haigha," Virgil said. He pronounced it to rhyme with 'mayor'. "He strolls along behind and enjoys the carnage, calling the soldiers back if he doesn't see enough desolation to please the *Big Boss Down Under*."

"I wish we could destroy them all," Dana said.

"We all do. I wish they had less than misery, less than pain, and more at the same time," Virgil said.

"How eloquent, Vine," a thunderous voice scared us. Cassie cringed and scooted behind Coral.

"What do you want, Belial?"

The man smiled. His hair was darker than Virgil's and was bluish black, his skin was tanned and tight, his body was lean, but powerfully built, and his face was more than handsome; it was beautiful. He moved with grace and confidence. He smiled again, blinding us with all the white teeth, and his green eyes sparkled and glittered, "I waited a while as I have known for some time you were about. Hello, lovely Alice."

"Go away," Virgil warned Belial.

"Oh, Vine, how silly. You see, I have come for her, the beautiful Alice, and she is now my prisoner. Let's see how your precious mission goes."

I couldn't help but notice his muscles rippling beneath the reddish leather, the tight shirt and tight leather pants he wore over black boots. He looked like a red knight or the red Greek god, come to face us.

The air around me seemed to ripple in waves. I saw it and felt it. My ears popped painfully, and I noticed Virgil; his black leathers looked tighter and stronger, more muscle-bound; he was so beautiful in body. His blue eyes lit up with a blaze against his pale skin. Even I could not look stare into those eyes of fire for more than a second.

Virgil, or rather Vine, as this was more his true form, or as much as we humans could discern, had pale skin, black ripples, blue fire. In those seconds, he wasn't the man I knew and loved, but a being so far removed from my understanding that my mind struggled to keep him in my sights. My view slipped and slid. Only as a fallen angel was he available for my love, normally he would be impossible to fathom.

Oh my, but he was a handsome man. A beautiful angel.

"You will not touch her, Belial," Virgil said, his voice low and like thunder so that a human ear could almost not comprehend.

"Alice," Belial said softly, purring, "take my hand; be my prisoner…a turn of a phrase really…my princess is more correct, my queen…my goddess…and let me love you."

"Like hell. Literally," I said. He didn't interest me in the least.

Ellie whispered, "Ohhh, ask me; ask me."

I wanted to hit her again.

"Okay, then let me do this. With my status and connections, I am in good with Lucifer, (all hail his glory). I can work out something so maybe Ole Vine can keep you here forever, and you and he could have a good life."

"Ha, good? Do I look stupid?"

"You don't; she does; he does," Belial said, pointing to Ellie and Cory. Coral snickered, despite the dire circumstances.

"You're an ass," Ellie told him.

Belial laughed lightly, "It could be good. You and Vine might live in a castle and have every desire met. You could have children…oh, not the ones with the souls, silly souls at that, but you could have a family and stay with him always."

Virgil roared his answer, "No, she'll not stay in this pit of ruin."

"I would make a deal if the dealer spoke honestly. You are a liar. I say no to every offer you have," I said.

"You should have taken the offer with me as my love," Belial made kissing sounds.

"Come on," Virgil roared.

Cory grabbed me to put my face against his chest so I couldn't see the fights as the Red Knight lunged at Virgil, my White Knight, sword slashing. My tears soaked Cory's shirt, but I saw none of the fight. Each time Cory grunted or groaned, a fresh stream of tears fell from my eyes, but if Virgil faltered or ducked a blow, I would scream and throw him off his game. If I watched and reacted, I could cause him to lose the battle.

"Holy shit," Cory yelped.

I turned to watch, biting my cheek. Virgil was strong, and the fight was equal so far, but Belial was very strong, filled with wickedness; he was like a summer rattler, swollen with poison and very dangerous. If Virgil didn't feint, one blow of Belial's sword would kill the man I loved and might cause the dead to walk the earth.

The fight was fair.

Danny didn't want it to be fair but wanted to win and send Belial packing. Limmerfer ran across the battlefield, distracting Belial for a fraction of a second, and Danny, *Dantanian,* suddenly didn't have the long rabbit teeth or the twitchy ear. He didn't move with a silly hop. He stood straight and looked beautiful, too. He was in his true form.

Dana gasped.

Dantanian took up his sword and swung it heavily at Belial, catching the demon off guard so that Virgil could swing his sword at his adversary. The cut into Belials' body sent fire and lightning in all directions, and his roar shook the ground like an earthquake. He backed away, furious, "You will beg me. Mark my words. You will beg."

In a moment, he was gone, and Danny heaved a sigh of relief, gasping for air. Virgil slid to the ground, and I ran to him. He said he was all right but was exhausted. The fight here in hell had weakened his spirit and tired him.I made him lean on me to walk and demanded we find a place to rest the remainder of the day and night.

Danny led us along a new trail. We found a medium-sized, but lovely mansion on a hill, overlooking a frozen pond that glistened. Danny spoke with the owner, and she abruptly threw open her door and exclaimed, "Alice!" But then she ignored me except for a smile and then scooped up Limmerfer into her arms, speaking baby talk to him, scratching and kissing his face and chin.

He grinned happily.

We had been led to a piece of paradise in hell.

CHAPTER THIRTY-SEVEN: RINGS AND PROMISES

Her hair was white-blonde, her sky blue eyes were crystal clear, and her skin was snowy skin; she wore a dress dotted with diamonds. She was ice and snow. She was the White Queen and beautiful. I let Coral hold Virgil and curtsied. Dana and Cassie did the same, and the men gave her little bows.

Only Ellie ignored the Queen, rolling her eyes instead. I made a mental note to slap Ellie later.

Limmerfer curled and purred happily as he became the center of attention with promises made of a fresh fish dinner for him. The cat was so spoiled.

"Come in, come in. We'll sooth your aches and put balm on your wounds. You'll get good meals and sleep in beds filled with soft feathers, and we'll have you feeling better fast. Let me get my servants to prepare your baths and then bring your silk robes." She called her army of servants and gave them orders.

"So, as I understand this, Alice has my ring, but I need to wear it, and then after this last circle of hell, we go out a doorway, and we are back to normal, right?" Ellie asked.

"That's what we understand," Cory said.

"Because I can't leave without the ring?"

"Right."

Ellie nodded to Cory, "I'm glad you brought the ring, then."

"Alice brought it," Danny mentioned as he walked by.

"That one?" Ellie pointed to the one I wore on my right hand, the one meant for her.

"This is the one I was given to bring," I said.

"Can I have it now? Do I have to wait?" she asked Virgil.

"Any time she wants to hand it over is fine. Or not at all. It's free choice."

Ellie held her hand out, "I'm ready."

Want to think I am mean hearted? That's fine, but I'm not. I am tender hearted and caring. At least, I had learned to be more so. I could show empathy and compassion, but I hesitated to hand her that ring. Granted, the mission was clearly stated that I was to retrieve a mortal who was wrongly in hell and deserved a chance to set everything right. Ellie was said to be that mortal. Only a mortal could be released, not a soul doomed to hell, a fallen angel, or a demon.

Those were the rules. I understood them.

"Imagine the earth populated by the walking dead because I stayed here and hell was too full. Can you grasp how horrible that would be? The zombies would eat people alive, ripping and tearing, and Alice, I bet you have parents there."

I looked at her.

"What would your poor parents do? What kind of world would it if the dead walked the earth? " Ellie said.It was a veiled threat.

"Horrible," I muttered.

She waved her hand a little at me, "So, I need my ring."

I might have handed it to her, but the word '*my*' bothered me. Was it her ring? Or was it mine to give? I had free choice. It was still my ring so far, and I had to do everything right here in hell. It was my duty to the world.

"Alice? My ring, please?"

"To be honest, I am not sure that this is the time to hand it over. In fact, if you don't stop pissing me off, you won't get it at all." That wasn't the best response, but it was exactly how I felt.

Ellie recoiled as if I had hit her. Again.

"She can't do this, can she?"

Virgil raised his eyebrows at Ellie and then at me, "Yes, she can. I can't say we expected it per se, but it was always possible. She didn't say she wouldn't for sure."

"But this is about me. Getting me out. Me being the mortal to get free," Ellie said angrily.

"I would have to review the contract and circumstances again to know that for sure. Granted, I came here for that, but things are not quite as we expected. I want to be sure I do everything correctly," I said a little spitefully.

"We don't want the dead walking the earth," Dana said softly.

"And do you know another mortal down here? Beside you?" Ellie asked.

"No. Are there more?" I asked Virgil.

"Stop asking to see if you have choices. It's about me," Ellie said.

Virgil shook his head, "Only Ellie."

"What a shame," I said.

She held her hand out again, "Alice, just do what you were sent to do. Let me have the ring so I can leave with all of you and the world will be saved."

"Not now," I set my jaw firmly. I had more questions and needed time to think this over. If Ellie didn't belong here now, I had a suspicion she would later in her life anyway. She hadn't learned much. I left her sitting in the parlor, and in a few minutes, she was alone, as everyone deserted her.

"She's not a very nice person, Virgil." I tucked him into the bed after a hot bath. He was still tired, and we planned to stay here two nights so he would be strong again. In the open, if Belial appeared again, we might find ourselves taken as prisoners if we weren't all recovered and able to fight. Even if we faced dogs or crazed prostitutes again, we needed every able person to fight.

"No, she isn't. She is the only mortal though. Use your common sense and heart to decide what to do," Virgil told me.

"She is just a vile person, and I need to think about her more. The ring is too precious to be handed over without thought."

"Why do you think you were chosen? To know those things."

I frowned, "I was very uninterested and complacent when we met. I was shallow."

"And look at yourself now. You have come a long way. You have changed a lot. Did you ever consider that is the real mission here?"

"What?"

Virgil pretended to fall asleep and said, "Think about it. Think what the real mission here was. Sacrifice, learning, interest, justice, love, friendship...they all matter."

Chapter Thirty-Eight: Dead Walking

There are many unsavory ways to be awakened in the wee hours of the morning. We were awakened by the sounds of gunshots and a moaning that chilled me to the bone. Had I not heard that moaning in movies? Had that very sound not frightened me when watching zombie flicks?

I told Virgil I would check it out and that he had should rest. I yanked on a robe and ran for the door where my other friends were getting prepared to open the front door. I asked Cassie to watch over Virgil since he was still weak.

As soon as we hit the ground outside, we were running.

Dozens of creatures came from the path, and they were moaning, drooling, dripping fluids, and powder or not, I could smell their waste and rot all around. Some of the humans, because they were people but dead ones, had fingers, hands, and arms missing. Weeping sores were left behind when parts were bitten or torn away and never healed.

I kicked one in the head as I swung my sword at a second one, removing his head. Before I could finish it off with a stab into its eye socket, I had to put the other zombie down. Sweeech was the noise my sword made as I drove into an eye and to the back of the skull. I was then able to stab the head on the ground until it stopped blinking and batting its eyes.

Coral, Dana, Cory, and Danny were just as busy as I was.

There were two men shooting their old-fashioned guns and dropping zombies with us. I made a guess that they were the two guides we were waiting for to lead us through the final circle of hell.

One was tall, wore a black cowboy, felt hat, a long black duster, black pants, string tie, and a crisp white shirt. He fired fast, reloaded, twirled his gun, and fired again. I saw, in a brief second, his gun had his initials set into the butt: WE.

Unlike WE and his rugged, handsome face, the other man, while also attractive, was a little shorter, had dark hair as well as blackberry eyes, and a wickedly happy grin on his face. He wore a similar outfit but used a rifle and a big knife to kill the undead.

Dana, on her back, kicked a huge man off her and to the ground; she pounced, stabbing him in his eyes. Coral was almost to her side to help, but seeing she had the fight under control, he spun to take down two zombies at once, smashing their heads in. The reek of their dead brains was appalling.

The tall gunfighter shot a zombie that ran at me.

"They aren't supposed to run," I grumbled.

"Why?" he asked, "you might wanna...you're showing."

My face burned red as I pulled my robe closed, embarrassed. I said, "I mean I didn't think they could run."

"So it seems they can," the other man said, "good luck we were headed this way. Hello, Dantanian."

Danny shook hands with the two men and said, "Wyatt, Doc, meet Cory, Coral, Alice, and Dana."

"Wyatt...Earp?" Danna asked her eyes wide.

He tipped his hat.

"Doctor John Henry Holliday, at your service," the second man spoke.

"Why are they in hell?" I asked, shocked again by something down here.

Holliday chuckled, "Those stages didn't rob themselves, and at the O K Corral...ummm...we kind of helped set that up and fired first. We regretted it. Wyatt did in particular, but we didn't regret it enough to make it right."

"They live far away in the better area, like where we arrived, but we just now needed them. They have it far less bad than most," Danny said.

Cassie looked out, saw we were all right, waved a few legs, and went back to tell Virgil we were fine.

"Are you here to be our guides?" Coral asked.

"Yup," Doc said, "sorry we're late. The roads are a mess. Seems you made Belial furious. These things are courtesy of him."

"I'm glad you were late. They could have broken in without our hearing. I didn't hear anything before your gunshots," Danny admitted.

Inside the big house, the White Queen was out of bed, wearing a thin robe over her sexy sleepwear, and said, "Hello, Doc."

"Hello, Thelma. Looking good."

"So are you. I saved you a warm spot in bed."

Doc followed her to her bed happily.

On the sofa, Ellie looked up at Wyatt Earp and yawned with boredom, "All done?"

"Yes. Thanks for the help," I snapped.

"I'm not much at fighting. Alice, what if you had been bitten, died, and turned? How would I get my ring?"

"I am selfish that way, huh?" I turned and left her, washed up, and climbed back in bed to sleep. Virgil turned over in his sleep, and I snuggled against his back. Each time I didn't throttle Ellie, I thought I should get a prize.

Virgil only awoke to use the facilities, to eat meals I brought him on trays, and to make sure I was unharmed. Limmerfer and I played; I tossed the ball, and he ran for it and brought it to me. More than anything, I avoided Ellie and spent time sitting alone with Limmerfer, thinking. There was a great spot on the third floor in a small alcove where I sat in a window seat wrapped in a soft blanket.

Limmy purred happily as I thought about everything I had been through and all I had seen and done. I tried to see Ellie from other points of view and attempted to be neutral. As I scratched Limmy's ears, I saw that his iolite stone set into his necklace or collar looked shiny and bright. Virgil's and Danny's were too small for them to travel back to my world; the stones were so tiny they were about to wink out.

My iolite was exactly as it had always been.

Only a mortal could pass from hell, and Ellie was the only mortal and the one we had been sent to rescue. I was sent here for a reason. It occurred to me that I did know what was right; whether I liked my choices or not, I had to follow the rules, and I had to be just.

"Fine, Limmy, what has to be…has to be. Demons lie, and angels are honest, and that's a fact that we'll have to live with," I said, scooping up my furry friend.

At dinner, Coral asked if I had good luck with all my thoughts during the day. I said I had excellent luck and that when we reached the final circle of hell, the ninth, I would do as I was supposed to do and give the ring to whomever it belonged.

Ellie sighed and smiled. I glared at her.

Chapter Thirty-Nine: The Ninth Circle of Hell

I didn't know what to expect as we left, bidding the White Queen goodbye. In some ways, this trip had taken forever, but now it seemed everything had gone by way too fast for me to grasp all the details. The zombie corpses littered the lawn, and the Queen said she would have her servants remove them.

We had fared well with the zombies, but if we hadn't been trained or prepared, we would have been torn apart and eaten alive right in the house. Here, in hell, that was normal. I had no idea how anyone became used to this.

Dana kept the gunfighters talking. She wanted to know all kinds of historical secrets, and I could almost imagine her taking mental notes for a book she wanted to write one day. She was fascinated with their stories and getting to meet two men from the past that she had only read about or seen portrayed in movies.

Although I had never noticed the slight lines of worry Dana wore on her face since she had been ill from the botched medical treatment and the guilt in her eyes before we came here, I now easily saw that those were no longer there. I could see they were absent. She smiled brighter and was at peace; confession and forgiving her own mistakes had been all she needed.

Coral was still Coral, but he looked lighter.

Cory looked more pale and frowned a lot, as if he had a lot on his mind.

I wondered if I looked more at peace. I would be once this mission was finished. Maybe. I wasn't sure because I would lose Virgil.

Before I could think more, a dozen creatures came at us from the rocks, dropping to their feet. They had human bodies, as far as shape, but thick scales covered their flesh, and their feet and hands were claw-like, sharp, and dangerous. Their heads were without real foreheads or chins, and their faces stuck out like a muzzle or a snout; their eyes were yellow and reptilian; small, sharp teeth filled their mouths.

Virgil and Danny both swung their swords, slashing away arms and heads. Wyatt and Doc both proved to be excellent sharpshooters as they took down all the lizard men who stood on the rocks around us, ready to attack. They bled greenish ichor.

I slammed my sword into the body of a lizard, but my sword bounced off. I had to step forward and put weight into my blow before I could cut him down. Cory and Dana had the same problem, but big Coral was lopping off heads with ease. Cassie had a knife that she used to finish off the ones we chopped and smashed to the ground.

This was just another test and attempt to stop us from finishing our mission, and it felt very petty to have lizard men fight a battle. They made a horrendous mewling noise when injured. Limmerfer had one in his claws, ripping and slashing after Coral had taken off the creature's arms. Limmy dug in, went for the eyes, and made a mess of the thing's face; Cassie finished it off and hugged the cat.

"Cassie and I always pull through," Cory said as he put his arm about her shoulders.It was a little strange to see the wild surfer-boy with an arm around a caterpillar, but Cassie was special.

"I detest these things," Coral kicked at a body, "lizards of all things. They think they're special 'cause they have scales? Well. I guess a cat whipped your scaly ass." He kicked again.

I knew Coral was feeling the stress of the mission coming to a close and having no idea what we were going to do or what was going to happen. I felt the same way. Dana gave my hand a squeeze to let me know she was nervous, too, but had faith we would be okay. We waited a few seconds while Lim cleaned his face and paws.

"Good shooting," I told Wyatt and Doc.

"Thank ya, Ma'am. We try," Doc told me and coughed a little. He and Earp were likable characters, well mannered and engaging to talk with. I hoped they would have a better time here than some did.

"Through here," Danny showed us. We followed him along the trail, under rock formations and into cold caverns that looked ancient. We had to climb up a few bluffs and then climb down, crawl under strangely canted boulders and around slippery slopes.

"I always thought hell was a burning fire pit," Coral noted, "I mean that's what I imagined and what the preacher man said; this is strange."

"That's a common misconception, but if you have ever been encased in ice, you'd know that ice is highly painful as well. Being cold may seem better as people can fall asleep and pass on, but the feel of ice against nerves hurts terribly," Danny said.

"I can't say I'd like either one," Coral noted.

"Remember, Satan is the father of lies. Be careful what you believe, and Danny and I can help less with advice here because it is his realm, and at this point, Alice, you must use free will and your own conscience to decide everything," Virgil said.

"But I need advice," I said.

"We can't help. You are going to step up and make choices, and you will do what is right. Alice, you were chosen for this for a reason. You can do this. Do you think we would have chosen someone who wasn't able to make hard decisions?"

I squeezed Virgil's hand in thanks. He was a mighty warrior, and he believed in *me*.

"Can I have my ring?" Ellie whined.

I ignored her.

"Alice?"

"Stop pestering me, Ellie," I hissed.

The room was cave-like, with obsidian stalagmites and stalactites that soaked up light. A pool of ice and rocks were set in the center of the room, and a beast with horns, many spidery eyes, and flapping wings struggled to emerge but was held tightly in the frozen mire. He eternally fought to be free, with no results.

As we entered the room, the beast, Satan morphed into a human, even more handsome, hiding his multiple eyes and trying to look like the Morning Star angel that he had once been. Satan was all lies. Hiding his ugliness was a trick to make us feel more secure.

I met him with sword in my hand. I wasn't tricked by the change in his looks.

"You don't need that sword. I'm no threat."

"Really? If you were so great and no threat, then no one here would be in misery and suffering. Even in my world, we fear you getting loose." I said, "I think you are a threat to everyone and everything."

Satan laughed charmingly, "How silly. I doubt I could get free unless...well...if you gave me that lovely ring...."

"You can't use it. You aren't a mortal."

"I could become a mortal and leave, or I could remain a god and be free of the ice and reign here as is my right," he said as he frowned.

"I think I'll keep it with me," I said. He could do those two things, I believed. Maybe for once he was telling the truth. His threats set some ideas in motion in my head.

He looked with longing at the ring on my hand. He wanted the iolite so badly that it was in his eyes: the desire.

"I couldn't tempt you with power or something fun like that?" Satan asked.

"No," I said, "I don't need power, and from what we've seen down here, trading my soul doesn't look like a very good deal. If you weren't trapped in the ice, you might get more respect when you make offers...just saying...."

Dana snickered.

Satan sighed, "I can see that point. Well, let's see what else might tempt you. Your friends' slates, you might want those wiped clean of any wrong deeds?"

"They are clean. At least Coral's is and Dana's. Besides, you don't do that. You don't have the power. They handled those things for themselves. Free will? Ring a bell?" he asked. He could turn on the charm, I noticed. It didn't affect me.

I looked at Cory pointedly because I didn't say his was clean.

Cory looked cross and said, "Just because I don't choose to air my dirty laundry here doesn't mean anything."

Satan sniffed, "I don't smell repentance."

"I don't smell your freedom," Cory snapped at Satan.

To the side, Belial clicked and clacked his talons at us, grinning and leering. He was enjoying this too much to attack, yet. Playing with his prey was enjoyable, and he didn't think his side could lose. I hated the way he drooled when he glanced at me, and it was all Virgil could do to keep from cutting him to ribbons.

I thought of him as the pervert demon.

Astaroth lounged on a rock, picking his teeth and preening since he was a Grand Duke and thought it was nice to rule in hell as opposed to serving in Heaven. I wondered if he really thought those warts and the fleas I saw on him were worth his choice and almost laughed as I watched him scratch absently at the bites. His feathers were a little tattered, and his naked form was unimpressive.

He was the homely demon.

Samael, the blind demon, ignored us but moved in the shadows. Virgil had warned me of him. He was the Angel of Death, and sometimes did good deeds but was always trying to tempt the humans. He was one of the more clever of the group.

He was the sneaky demon.

"How's Lilith, Samael? Keeping you busy?" Danny asked with a chuckle.

"She's a keeper," Samael responded with good humor, "I sure wish you'd settle this another way and let me have at my business collecting souls and...ummm...I am so hungry for fresh souls. It would be delicious."

He supposedly was the one who tempted Eve and later married Lilith, Adam's first wife who was too prideful. I didn't understand all of that: what was true and what was legend, but he was one creepy demon with impressive horns and full, flappy wings. He was one of the trickiest of all.

I could be cheeky and hold my own. However, I was careful not to push too hard since Danny and Virgil could barely hope to hold back one demon each, and my friends and I couldn't hold back one demon of this strength together. They were only holding back because I had to give the gemstone away; they couldn't just take it from me.

"So before you head back to your world, we have business, Alice?" Satan asked.

No lie, to have Satan speak my name left my legs like jelly. I was scared. Of everything I had seen or done, this was the most terrifying of all. Even in human form, he was terrifying, and I shivered. He was of nightmares and pure evil.

"Gimme the ring," Ellie demanded. Same song. Same tune.

"Maybe, we should just feast," Belial said. His infernal brethren giggled.

If they chose, they could eat us all. There would be a fight, but I wouldn't bet on my side to win. Samael alone controlled over two thousand demons.

A light began to shine in a corner, dancing around, then blazing, and in a few seconds, the brightest light appeared and then faded.Now, we could uncover our eyes and look at who had come to visit. Danny and Virgil didn't look surprised at all at the newcomer.

They expected him.

The air rippled and danced, like when Virgil took his true form, but more so. My ears ached as if my eardrums were bursting and as if all the oxygen were being sucked out of the cavern for a second; we gulped for air.A man appeared who was muscled and goldenly beautiful, who stood straight and powerful, and who had a handsome, albeit sad, golden-toned face beneath sunlight-golden, shining curls. He wore armor of pure silver over a short, soft white tunic that was trimmed in purple silk.

Along his side, he griped a magnificent sword more than twice as heavy and as long as the one I carried, maybe three times! It was shining silver, and its hilt was garnished by an intricately wrought design of swirls and dotted with large rubies, diamonds, and emeralds. An amethyst glittered from the end, next to his hand. I don't know how I knew, but I felt his sword might be what we call radioactive; it wouldn't harm him, but it would the demons, and we couldn't hold it.

Virgil and Danny inclined their heads to the new angel.

I didn't know if I should curtsy or what, but I dipped down, and Dana and Cassie did the same. Coral bowed his head in a greeting. What was proper protocol when meeting a major angel, I didn't know. I do know I met him with my jaw hanging open and with my eyes wide.

Belial, Astaroth, and Samael hissed and spat angrily while Satan howled. They weren't happy to see the new arrival.

"Why did you come here, Michael?" Satan demanded. He screeched so loudly that my ears hurt again.

"Because we have deals to be brokered, exchanges to be made, and justice to be served. Why else would I suffer the pain of having to come here? Only the fate of a world He loves so much would cause Him to send me here. Again," Michael said.

Virgil said that long ago, Michael and other good angels had beaten back the evil, prideful ones and sent them here. A third were sent crashing to the earth as Michael defended Heaven.Michael's battle with Satan, called Lucifer then, was a long, brutal war. The planet Mars, part of the battleground where the worst of the fighting went on, was still desolate and ruined, pitted by the great falls the fighting angels took and was still forever stained with their blood. It is said Mars still has rocks that were sheared off by Michael's sword.

"Yeah, I was getting my second wind when he stabbed me," Satan bragged, "I could have taken you, Michael."

We ignored him as Michael looked at me.

"Alice, we of the Seraphim appreciate that you care for others and your world so much that you agreed to take on this mission which could not have been pleasant for you and your loyal friends. Your unselfishness is commendable. We were most disturbed when this disgusting being grabbed a mortal who was not meant for hell," Michael pointed to Ellie.

"Meh...if you knew her, you'd see why I grabbed her; she wouldn't have passed."

"But you were not allowed. She had to be judged, just like everyone else," Michael told Satan.

"I heard she was the final one. The dead will walk the earth if she remains because hell is full at the time," I said.

"That is all true. One mortal less must be here so all can be set to right again. After that, there will be more than enough room for souls to come here for the next few hundred thousand years. And sadly, they will come here."

I thought quickly. If she, Ellie, left with us and if she were in fact doomed to hell after she died again, then maybe it would be a retrograde event? Would her soul again be one too many? Did it work that way? I don't know theology. I would gladly stay here than subject my world and my parents to the living dead walking the earth.

I couldn't take that chance, could I?

Ellie muttered I was a bitch, as I said that aloud. That answered my question. She was not a very good person; she couldn't be allowed to waltz away when souls such as Earp's and Holliday's, the White Queen's, and Cassie's were trapped here. It wasn't right.

But as I said that part aloud, I handed the silver and iolite ring to Ellie. "I had a mission, but the mission wasn't to take it upon myself to be the judge. I can't judge you, Ellie." She didn't notice the ring looked a little differently.

Dana groaned.

Coral shook his head, understanding, but not liking my choice.

Cory said I was an idiot.

Ellie yipped with happiness as she slid the ring on and smiled, but the smile turned into a twisting of her mouth, and she screamed; peals of noise were a barrage we could barely stand. In the blinking of an eye, Ellie shriveled to a husk, turned to dust, and fell to the ground where frigid, wet breezes blew her corporal body-dust away. The ring fell, and I scooped it back into my hand before one of the demons could get it as Michael used his sword to keep them at bay.

"What happened?" Dana asked, almost screaming. Cassie ducked behind Coral. I was glad I had grabbed the ring when I did, without thinking, because if I had to now, I would be too terrified to go near the pile of greasy dust.

"Don't fear, Cassie, you are safe," Michael said.

"Ellie wasn't good, Alice, but a deal was a deal as she hadn't been properly judged before she was grabbed and taken here. I believe she has now been judged with Michael here," Virgil said.

"She was bad?"

"Very, but you were smart and used your conscience, Alice. It wasn't your place to judge but to do as asked. I am pleased you made the right choice," Michael told me.

I thanked him. It was mega cool to be praised by an angel.

"She has gone on to the proper realm for her punishment. Unless I am off in my guess, I think she may have gone to the Land of the Lepers for being a disease on society?" Michael asked.

Samael chuckled, "Another leper…such a petty position for her, but she may have gone to the dysentery section, considering how she talked."

"She'll stay here? There? She is there now? " I asked.

"Yes. Her body fell apart, and she is there now. If an undeserving one wears the ring, he or she falls to dust and has a new body as you have seen."

"Then why do you lust after my ring? You'd fall to dust, too."

Samael shook his head, "No, because I am a demon…that's for mortals."

Satan grinned at us, "But we have the same problem, again, don't we, Alice? One too many stuck here."

"She still counts?" Coral asked.

"Yes, she does," Satan sneered, "more than ever she does. She removes any doubt really. We could march on earth right now…."

"It's getting time for all of you to go, Alice," Michael told me.

"But…."I thought about what this meant. Dead walking free? Doc and Wyatt Earp looked at me. Coral and Dan watched me. Every eye was on me. "It's all about math, and I was never great at math, but that's what this is."

"Math?" Michael asked.

We saw the opening back to our world. It was a hole in the wall that glowed with a brilliant blue-purple light. I sighed, "Coral, you and Dana go on. You need to return to our world where things make sense and it's safer."

"What about…?" Coral began, but he knew the time to give me advice was gone. I had to be the grown up and make hard choices, now. He smiled, and I felt he was proud of me that I had grown up a little, and he was pleased.

"And Wyatt and Doc, thank you for your help. I hope you find peace," I told them.

'Alice?" Cory spoke, "Ummm…this is going to sound really weird, but I want to stay. I know it's crazy, but Cassie needs me here, and we make a good team, and face it, I'm coming here eventually anyway."

"You can't do that. How do you know?"

"Because I killed a man when I was thirteen and did seven years in juvenile prison. I beat him to death with my hands because he touched my sister in a sex way. The right thing to do would be to forgive maybe or to regret killing him or to be sorry I lost my temper and did it. I beat the guy with him, too, and he didn't do anything; he was just there when I was angry. He is in a home now...drools and sits all day like a vegetable...and you know what? I'm not sorry at all."

I took a deep breath, "Oh Cory...."

"Really. No regrets. I'd do it again. Maybe I'll find the guy who did it down here and beat the shit out of him again. Maybe Cassie and I will smoke hashish and eat magic mushrooms, but I'm headed here anyway. Right, Michael?"

Michael hung his head.

My throat tightened with sadness.

"Where are Pax and Annie now?" I asked.

"Heaven."

"And Dinah?" I asked that as well.

"She wasn't born with a soul. She is...she isn't...."

"So she wasn't sentenced to hell? That's the key. One has to be sentenced here and be mortal. Someone can't be here and remain; he has to be judged by you, Michael, and then you get their souls or Mr. Six-Eyes gets them."

Satan spit.

" Then, they can leave this place with the silver and iolite if they are mortal. And then they will have a change to live and be judged. I choose to put the ring on Dinah. Give her a soul, and bring her here; she will have a life with me. It fits the rules. She never got a soul and hasn't lived or had a chance for judgment."

Michael and Satan both looked at me as if I were insane.

"You can't do that. She...she isn't...well...she was...." Satan faltered.

"I can. It follows the rules. She was condemned to be here," I said.

"I am the Angel of Life and Death, and a mortal may pass through. Dinah was never given a soul, but if she had, then she is mortal and has free will and cannot be condemned to hell as she has not lived and been judged," Michael kind of spoke to himself.

Wyatt and Doc walked out of the cavern, and I heard murmuring. Amid some surprised voices, Astaroth lunged at Michael, but one poke with Michael's sword and the demon whined and scooted away, his chest burned badly. From where the gunslingers had retreated, Dinah walked into the cavern, whimpering when she saw the demons. Cassie and I grabbed her quickly and soothed her fears, promising she was safe. Poor thing. The last she remembered was being mauled by a dog and not being in a cavern with devils.

I handed Limmy to her, and although he was big in her arms, he was like a warm blanket that warmed her, and his purr calmed her at once. She held him tightly, and he seemed delighted.

"Good call, Alice," Danny said, his one eye winking at me, "come on, and be done. I have other missions awaiting me, you know. And you know I'm stuck here a while longer since I love my work way too much. Recall, I warned you about enjoying the work too much." He gave Cory a small smile to let Cory know he understood; Danny was empathetic.

I knew what Dantanian was saying to me. He was giving me his blessings for the next part. He patted his pocket and winked at me. Since Cory was staying, I had two mortals to take out, and Dinah filled one space. If I wanted to save the world, I had a second space to fill.

"I have the other one…if the person wishes."

"You can't. You used your silver ring and stone for the child. You and she will be fighting my minions when we come into your world. Ummm, Tasty," Satan said, chuckling.

I held something out for him to see. The ring was two bands, if you recall, and although it took some work, I separated them, sticking them back for Ellie with a bit of tar from the sole of my boot. Now, I showed them that Dinah wore one band with the iolite set into it. I had the empty band and the little sticky bit of tar, just in case.

The other band was in my hand.

Michael looked puzzled.

Danny handed me something he had kept all this time: the huge iolite gem he had gotten from the Duchess. It glittered and danced in the firelight. The demons all took notice. It was large enough and powerful enough to set free a whole busload of demons, souls or not. It would open the doorway fully.

I whispered and told Dinah to go along and find Coral and Dana.

"You hold a great deal of power, Alice. What will you do with that?"

The demons called out promises and trades for the gem, for they couldn't take it from my hand. They could grab one of my friends and threaten to harm him, but then I would use the stone to blow them to pieces. The stone had the power to release Satan from his prison of ice; all of the demons could all have free reign again. With this, I could burn away a full quarter of hell if I wanted. So many choices lay before me

I said, "Virgil came here as an angel. He was another being. I want him as a mortal with a soul. I want him to come with me if he wants."

"Impossible," Satan snapped. The others mumbled obscenities.

"He could. He was sent here as an angel. He could become mortal and leave," Cory nodded, and Cassie agreed, "He can't leave as an angel, but he can leave as a man with the iolite."

"Those aren't the rules. Getting that girl was stretching things," Satan said, "You can't break the rules."

"You do. You always lie and trick people and break rules and slip under them. Well, I want to slide under a rule, too. I did the mission, and I deserve some sort of reward so it can all be packed into this request," I said, stomping my boot.

Satan sneered at me.

"And Dinah wasn't one of the dead or condemned here, so she was outside the rules. As for Virgil, he was here as one being, and he can convert to another since he has never been human and mortal."

"Do you know what you ask of him? He will suffer as a mortal, be judged when he dies, will lose his powers, will be nothing more than a human," Michael said.

"And didn't the angels get into trouble for not recognizing the goodness and wonder of humans?" I asked, "but it is Virgil's choice." I was scared of his answer. "Michael's argument was valid, and one day, Virgil could be an angel again. Would he want to be a mortal?But I am simply offering him the chance. If he can't go through the pain of change or doesn't want to go with me, then I will go on with my life. But I demand he have a choice."

"Demand?"

"Ask most humbly?" I backed down.

"Vine?"

"Yes. Yes, I wish to transform and give up my status to be a lowly human. I have discovered they are quite lovely, brilliant, and good hearted."

"Are you sure, Vine? Do you know the pain you will suffer?"

Vigil stared at the ground, "I know what the pain will be. I accept it gratefully."

"Bad pain? A lot?" I asked.

Satan chuckled, "Your Vine will scream with the pain."

"We're ready. Let's do this," Samael said, stretching. Behind him appeared other demons, and Dantanian prepared for battle. I barely had time to hug and kiss Cory and Cassie before Virgil pushed me to the opening to my world. I said, "I love you Cassie; take care of Cory."

"Love you, Alice. Thank you for bringing him to me."

"Go. The fight is nigh. God willing, I will join you, but I can't promise what will come out of the opening, so be ready," Vigil kissed me and pushed me harder. I managed a quick thanks to Michael and handed him the giant gemstone.

CHapter Forty: True Mission

I leaped head first into the hole, and Limmerfer leaped with me. I held him as we spiraled, seeing places we had been, frightening images of the past few days, and scenes of the future. I saw Cassie and Cory, hand in hand, eating mushrooms and dancing. They looked really happy. I saw their children, but hid my face in Limmy's soft fur since I just couldn't look at the progeny of human-caterpillar even if I did like them both. It was hell, but they were abiding their sentence, and it seemed okay. I hoped the kids kind of took after Cory, but at least they had a family. I thought Cory would be good to Cassie and treat her well. It was a feeling I had.

I trembled when I saw an image of what happened when I left the cavern.Astaroth, Samael, Belial, Wyrmwood, and Beelzebub, plus scores more of the demons, followed the orders of the hateful Satan and attacked Virgil, Danny, and Michael. Blood flew as claws and swords flashed. They so wanted the iolite. But it needed a silver band, and I had slipped that part to Virgil before I left. They might get the gem but would still be missing a part of the puzzle they needed.

My parents raised no fool.

I saw another battle. A woman was fighting with a huge sword of silver, slaying demons, setting fire to hell, burning away all the bad, and leaving some people in purgatory or in a kind of stasis but not in a place of torture and filth. I saw half of hell burned to ashes and the wicked destroyed forever. It seemed Cassie, Cory, and (oh, Lord, help us) a litter of caterpillar-surfers were watching.

The woman, tall and dark haired, was beautiful, strong, and excellent with her sword, able to flip and twist in mid-air, spin, and almost fly. She looked as powerful as any of the angels I had watched fight, but she was all innocence and peace. Cory and Cassie stood close to her and cheered. The vision faded.

If one of the demons got the gem, it would open the door to hell, and my world would be lost. I saw the possibility that demons might rule the earth, devouring innocents and spreading cruelty. That visage finally faded, too. That was terrible to see.

I saw Dantanian fighting in my dream like state. *'Use the vorpal sword to slay the jabberwocky* ', I heard as I spiraled to the bottom and onto the grass. I remembered how the White Queen gave Danny a special sword and wondered if it might be a *vorpal* sword. If so, they had a chance, not that I was sure what the word meant, but it sounded mighty.

There was Dinah, Coral, and Dana, all waiting for me. I was glad to see them, too. I intended to tell them, later about Cory, Cassie, and the Cory-pillar children.

I held my arms out, "My little girl, Dinah." And she ran to me to be held tightly and whispered she loved me. I held her and dimly wondered how I would explain that I suddenly had a child to care for, but I knew my parents would adore her.

We all looked to the hole in the ground. It blazed purple, and then it went dark. A hand appeared at the edge, and someone struggled.

I ran to help Virgil climb out. I soaked his shirt with tears as I wept from relief. The hole closed as we held one another. Dinah grabbed us both in her little arms.

"Stop crying. It's all done, now. Everything is set to rights. Alice, you were amazing."

"It's over?"

He tilted his head and got to his feet, weakly, "Sorry. I'm exhausted from the battle, and the pain of changing was…unique…like a blade so fine and sharp one can hardly feel it until a second later. But Danny held them back, and Saint Michael did some grievous damage before he left. Danny is fine."

"You made it through your mission," Coral grinned.

"With losses," I thought of sweet, brave Pax, kind Annie, and funny Cory and Cassie, the gunslingers, and the White Queen. I was so sleepy and tired that I lay down on the soft grass, with Dinah beside me, Limmerfer at my shoulder, and Virgil on the other side, "I saw strange things as I passed through to here," I said as I rested on the ground comfortably. I watched clouds.

"You saw the woman with a sword? The one who burns hell away and destroys the demons and has a great power?" Virgil asked.

"I did."

"That was our child. Wait; don't look so shocked. You know how odd things can be, and that is a long time from now. Danny will come get her for the greatest mission of all time. Only she can do those things. And she can only exist because I am here with you."

I cocked my head.

"This was your true mission, Alice. Your true mission was to make sure Kitty, or Katherine, will be borne of us." He kissed me and lay back to rest.

I began to slip into a deep sleep. I was tired and satisfied with my work, and all was right with the world. Limmerfer was purring; he was soft. A kitty. *Kitty. Vorpal sword. The King of Hearts and Tweedle Dee and Tweedle Dum, the March Hare and Mad Hatter, and a bunch of demons in the mix. The Duchess and the White Queen, the Red Queen, and a caterpillar.*

Dreaming.

"So, Alice," Dum had asked me at dinner, *"Have you considered that maybe you are at home, in bed asleep, and only dreaming all of this?"* That was confusing. Could that be true? Was that possible?

"It would be a long dream," I said in response.

"Dreams occur in a split second anyway. Maybe we are a part of your dream and you'll awaken and find this never happened," Dum had told me.

I dozed, and after some time, I began to emerge from dreams of where I had been and what I had seen. I emerged from the land of talking caterpillars and lice hookers and ugly centaurs. I was afraid.

I was almost fully awake now, but my eyes were still shut. I felt Limmy's fur next to me, and he still purred, but what if I had simply fallen asleep on the grass and dreamed? What if I opened my eyes and Virgil and Dinah were gone? My hell would be to look and find it all a dream.

But isn't that poetic?

Ever drifting down the stream—lingering in golden gleam—
Life, what is it, but a dream?

(Fort Worth2013)